"IT'S GONE!" EXCLAIMED TOM. "GONE!"

Tom Swift and his Television Detector.   *Frontispiece.*

TOM SWIFT AND HIS TELEVISION DETECTOR

OR
Trailing the Secret Plotters

By
VICTOR APPLETON

Author of
Tom Swift and His Motorcycle,
Tom Swift Among the Diamond Makers,
Tom Swift and His Sky Train,
The Don Sturdy Series,
Etc.

ILLUSTRATED BY
NAT FALK

NEW YORK
GROSSET & DUNLAP
PUBLISHERS

Made in the United States of America

CONTENTS

CONTENTS

TOM SWIFT AND HIS TELEVISION DETECTOR

CHAPTER I

IN THE SECRET VAULT

"WHAT are you doing, Ned?"

"Listen to this, Tom."

The youthful manager of the Swift Construction Company, of which the eminent but equally youthful Tom Swift was the head, touched some part of a small but complicated mechanism on the desk in front of him. At the other end of the room, seated at a table on which were piled numerous papers and blueprints and several strange looking models, was Tom Swift. He glanced with an amused smile toward his chum and helper.

"Well, I'm listening," said the young inventor. "Go on, Ned."

"Just a moment. This connection is a bit loose. If you had given me more help on this jigger—it's the only one I've ever tried to invent, Tom—it would work the first time, but as it is——"

The silence of the room which formed the entrance to Tom Swift's experimental laboratory was suddenly broken by a strange zizzing, buzzing and snapping sound. There was also a spitting of purplish-blue sparks, followed by a succession of broken impulses which anyone familiar with telegraphy would have translated into dots, dashes and spaces. Tom smiled a bit indulgently and asked:

"What are you doing with that old spark coil I rigged up for you, Ned?"

"You'll see what I'm trying to do as soon as it gets warmed up. As I said, if you'd given me more help on it——"

"I didn't mean to turn you down, Ned, when you asked me to look over some jigger you were working on. In the first place, I've a lot on my mind."

"I know it, Tom. You generally have. I'm not kicking. Only I say this would work better if you had given me some help. I'm not much on inventing. However, I think I have it going now."

"And in the second place," went on Tom, as if determined to justify his lack of interest in Ned's "invention" at which the young manager was tinkering, "there's something very special that I must figure out, so——"

"There she goes, Tom! I have it working now!" Ned interrupted, apparently with little regard for Tom's remarks. "See if you can pick it up."

Once more came those staccato snappings, buzzings and zizzings, separated into long and short impulses with spaces between them. Tom listened intently.

"It's some sort of a message, Ned," Tom said after a few seconds, "but it doesn't make sense. It's Morse code—dot and dash—and sounds like commercial coming in over the radio."

"That's right, Tom! I haven't forgotten how to send, I guess, nor you how to receive. Could you get the words, Tom?"

"Of course! But they're balderdash! No sense at all."

"Write 'em down, Tom, as you take them again and see what it makes," begged Ned.

More to please his manager than because he thought what Ned was doing would amount to anything, Tom took pencil and paper while his chum waited, preparing to send the strange message again. Though it seemed at the time to be but a scientific experiment, the hour was to come when it was to mean the difference between life and death.

"Ready, Tom?"

Again the blue and purple sparks, again the zizzling, the snapping and cracking. Tom Swift listened intently and then jotted down some words on the paper. As they formed before him his smile broadened though it was a tolerant manifestation of mirth. Ned Newton was a fine financial manager, but as an inventor of a new form of wireless sending apparatus—well, Tom Swift had his doubts. Nevertheless, the young inventor complied with his chum's wish.

The sparks ceased and the echoes of the snapping dots and dashes died away. Tom picked up the paper on which he had written the words that came to him through the air of the room in telegraphic fashion.

"What is it?" asked Ned, now smiling in his turn.

"Balderdash, just as I told you. There must be something mixed or scrambled somewhere, Ned. This is what I got: *Blime ʒax fernmo apentish wacko lushford.*"

"That's it, Tom! I see you haven't forgotten your Morse."

"Oh, that part is all right, though I'm not used to taking Welsh."

"Welsh!" repeated Ned.

"Yes, it reads like Welsh, or maybe it's Greek."

"No, it's English, Tom."

"English! Why, there's no sense in the words, Ned."

"Of course there isn't any as they stand,"

chuckled his chum. "It's a new code I'm getting up, just for use between you and me. Translated, my message would read: *I am in trouble —help me.*"

Tom studied over this for a moment. He looked at the strange words, then came over to Ned's desk to inspect the apparatus.

"Not a bad idea," admitted the young inventor. "A private code that you can use to communicate with me and I with you. You'll have to show me the system, though."

"Sure I will, Tom, as soon as it's perfected. This jigger seems to work all right now," and he indicated the machine on his desk.

"Oh, that's the small portable wireless set you had me make for you, Ned. I recognize it now. But what's the use of it? I mean, just at present. You aren't in trouble."

"No, but I might be some day—kidnapped, you know. If I then had my pocket wireless set with me, or could get at the key in a private station, I could send you a call for help in this code and you could come and rescue me."

"If I knew where you were, maybe I could," Tom chuckled. "But I'd have to invent some sort of detector to locate you, a kind of television detector, I guess we could call it. But why all this bosh about being kidnapped?"

"There's more of it going on, Tom, than you have any idea of," and Ned's voice was serious.

"Now that my sending jigger works, I'm going to perfect the secret code."

"Go ahead. It isn't a bad idea, though I don't believe we'll have much use of it in rescuing you from kidnappers."

"You never can tell, Tom. I hope I haven't bothered you too much with this little experiment of mine. You said you had something to puzzle over and——"

"I have, Ned. Something very important. I think this is the time to let you in on a secret that has been kept from you and everybody else for a long while. Now I'm going to tell you. It's a mighty important secret, Ned, so please see that all the doors and windows are secured. I don't want anyone to know about this. And you'd better send word to have Koku come and stand guard at the outer door."

"Gosh, you *are* getting spooky, Tom," chuckled Ned. "Well, I'll 'phone for your giant and then I'll be ready for the secret. I hope it will justify the veil of mystery you are draping about it."

"I think you will agree with me that it does, Ned. You shall judge as soon as Koku comes."

Koku, whose devotion to Tom Swift was slave-like, had been brought back from one of Tom's strange trips to a queer land, and though Koku the giant was as simple as a child in some matters, he had a herculean strength which had stood Tom in good stead more than once. A telephone message from Ned to the quarters of Koku brought the big man to the laboratory.

"Master want?" he asked, grinning broadly.

"Yes, Koku," answered the young inventor. "Stand outside the laboratory door and don't let anyone in unless I tell you to. It's very important," and Tom, to make sure Koku understood, added a few emphatic words in the giant's own tongue. Koku responded likewise and Ned asked:

"What did he say, Tom?"

"Well, it doesn't sound exactly pretty in English," was the answer, "but in effect Koku said if anyone tried to get in he would make his head grow where his feet are now."

"Bend him double, eh?"

"Something like that, yes. Well, now I guess we're ready, Ned."

Having made sure that no unauthorized person could gain access to the laboratory, and having convinced himself as to the security of doors and windows, and having looked out to note if Koku was on guard, Tom Swift slowly walked toward a picture of his father which hung on the wall of the laboratory. Lifting the portrait to one side, he pressed on a part of the panel exposed. There was a slight clicking noise and the floor beneath Ned's feet seemed to rumble and tremble.

"What's all this, Tom?" asked the manager in a loud voice. Though he and Tom were chums of many years' standing, Ned could not help but be impressed at this time with the young inventor's unusually solemn manner.

"I am opening the secret vault, Ned," Tom answered in a low voice.

"The secret vault! I didn't know you had one."

"No, I didn't intend that you should until the right time came. Now it has. It isn't that I didn't trust you, Ned," Tom went on earnestly, "but the fewer who know a secret the safer it is kept."

"Oh, I know that. I'm not at all put out. But a secret vault! Where?"

"Beneath the floor of this laboratory. I have started the mechanism working. You'll see the concealed staircase in a moment."

"Golly, Tom! This is like a movie!"

"That floor where you're standing is going to be moving in another second," Tom chuckled. "Better step back a bit, Ned."

The young manager did so, the wonder on his face growing as he felt the rumbling and trembling increasing. Suddenly part of the floor slid back, and there was revealed a flight of iron steps leading down into a dark hole.

"Why, Tom!" Ned exclaimed in astonishment, "I had no idea that this laboratory was over a secret staircase and vault. You have certainly hidden it well."

"I needed to, Ned. Some of my most important secrets are in this underground vault. I had it made the time the plant was temporarily shut down and you were on a vacation. Except for the few men who did the actual constructing and who are to be trusted, my father and I are the only ones who know about this vault. Now you know the secret, Ned, or you will when you go down these stairs. Come on. Don't be afraid. They're safe."

"But dark as a pocket, Tom."

Tom snapped a switch just under the edge of the opening in the floor and the staircase was illuminated. Wondering more and more, Ned followed his chum down, their heels clanking on the iron treads of the stairs.

The flight ended in a small, square vestibule made of solid concrete, and in the centre was a heavy steel door. Tom stood in front of this, touched a spring, or lever, which Ned did not notice, and the door slid back, revealing a small vault lined with shining steel like the strong room of a bank. On three sides were small niches, some closed with steel doors like those behind which renters of safety deposit boxes hide their valuables. A few of the niches were larger, and these contained models of strange machines which Ned Newton had never before seen.

"A few things I am working on," Tom remarked as he observed Ned's gaze on these models. "Some of them will be valuable in the course of years. The time isn't ripe yet to spring them."

"A lot of plans there, Tom," Ned remarked, pointing to some blueprints on a table at one side of the vault.

"Yes, some of them are valuable, too. But I didn't bring you down here to show you those. They're in the regular course of work, or will be some day. This is a greater and more terrible secret. I have kept it to myself long enough. I need to share it with someone. I'll make it all clear to you in a moment."

Tom Swift took a little key from his pocket and walked to a steel-doored niche in one corner of the vault. He opened the outer door, and revealed another within. This, too, swung back when a second key was inserted. Tom thrust his hand inside, felt around, then started back in surprise and consternation.

"It's gone!" he exclaimed. "Gone!"

"What?" asked Ned.

"The box containing the secret formula of one of the most deadly gases ever known! Oh, there'll be terrible trouble over this! Who could have robbed my secret vault?"

CHAPTER II

THE INTRUDER

Tom Swift grabbed up from the table, where many blueprints were scattered, a portable electric light. This he plugged into a socket, then inserted the bulb into the farthest corner of the interior of the secret niche. From where he stood Ned Newton could look within the tiny hiding place and see that it was empty.

"Yes, it's gone, all right," Tom said in a strained voice. "I was pretty sure it had been taken as soon as I put in my hand, but it was best to be absolutely certain. The secret formula is gone!"

"I haven't the least idea what you're talking about, Tom," Ned remarked, "but if it's something small it might have been put by mistake into some other niche or box. Why don't you take a look?"

"Because I'm sure, Ned, that it could be in no other place except this. If it isn't here—and it isn't—it's been taken. But that's not all."

"What do you mean, Tom?"

"I mean it's deplorable enough to think that

II

the secret of the deadly gas may be used by unscrupulous persons to snuff out many lives—that's bad in itself—but since one thing has been stolen from my secret vault, other things may also be missing. This upsets all my plans. I thought I had this place so well concealed that only a few trusted persons, including my father and myself, knew of it. But this hiding place must have become known, for otherwise access could not have been had here and the gas formula stolen. It's bad, Ned! Bad!"

"What's all this about a secret deadly gas, Tom? I didn't know you went in for that sort of thing."

"I don't. It was to prevent the stuff from ever being used that I so carefully hid the formula. Now it's gone. Well, there's no use in our staying down here. I'll look for clues a little later. Let's go up to the laboratory and I'll tell you all about it."

While the boys are ascending the stairs and preparing to shut the secret vault, I will take a brief moment to tell my readers something about Tom Swift and his wonderful achievements.

He lived with his aged father, Barton Swift, and the latter's housekeeper, Mrs. Baggert, in a fine house not far from the great plant of the Swift Construction Company. It is needless to mention that Tom's pretty young wife, who was Mary Nestor, also resided in the Swift home.

Koku the giant, and Eradicate, an eccentric and aged Negro, were part of the household, and there was intense jealousy between these two as to which one should most often serve their young master. Tom's mother had been dead a long time. Ned Newton, a boyhood chum and of late years Tom's financial manager, lived on the other side of the town of Shopton.

In the first volume of this series, "Tom Swift and His Motor Cycle," the reader is told how Tom started on his inventive career by the purchase of a motorcycle from Mr. Wakefield Damon of the neighboring town of Waterfield. Mr. Damon bought it for his own use, but when it tried to climb a tree with him the eccentric man, who was continually blessing something, sold the machine in disgust.

Tom repaired it, made it more speedy, and had some surprising adventures with it. From then on this lad did marvelous things with various machines. His motorboat, his airship, his submarine, and his electric runabout, to mention only a few, brought him further adventures. These were continued in his war tank, his sky train, and in the volume immediately preceding this one, entitled "Tom Swift and His Giant Magnet," is related the story of how he raised a sunken submarine when the government salvagers had failed.

Tom had only recently returned after completing this hazardous undertaking when he again plunged into the activities of some new inventive work. What this consisted of he had not mentioned to Ned Newton, and it was not until the episode of the secret code message and the visit to the looted vault that the young manager realized some new plan was afoot in Tom's career.

"I don't see how they did it! I don't see how they did it!" Tom murmured as he and his chum climbed up into the laboratory.

"Did what?" asked Ned.

"How they got into the vault in the first place," went on Tom. "It's a mystery I'll have to solve. And also I must get that formula back. It means death to many if it is in the hands of unscrupulous men, which I fear it is. That's why they stole it, though I don't see how. I must find it."

"This may be the first use you can make of your television detector, Tom," ventured Ned.

"What television detector? I haven't any such apparatus."

"I know you haven't, but when I was snapping out that secret code message a little while ago and said I might want to communicate with you if I were kidnapped, you said you'd first have to find me and might do it with a television detector."

"Oh, that—yes," and Tom smiled.

"You could make one, couldn't you, Tom?"

"I haven't really given it a thought. I just spoke on the spur of the moment. Of course, to find something secret, hidden, stolen or someone kidnapped some such apparatus would be invaluable. But it wouldn't be easy to construct."

"I've yet to see Tom Swift stop because a thing wasn't easy," spoke Ned, and his tone was sincere. "Now, this may be the very chance you need. Develop the television detector, Tom! After all, what is television?"

"Tele—afar," murmured Tom. "Vision—to see. To see something that is far off. You know how it's done, Ned. Light travels in waves. Waves are impulses. There are sound waves, light waves and electrical waves. In television, light waves transmitted from living persons moving in one room are sent through the ether in a sort of X-ray manner, are transformed into wireless electrical impulses, and so enter a suitable reproducing machine in another room, perhaps in a distant city. To enable the receiver to see the persons at a distance, the electrical impulses are transformd back again into light waves, and we have television."

"Just as you did it in your photo telephone, eh, Tom?"

"Something like that, Ned, yes."

"And as you did it in your talking pictures, where I performed some stunts in one room, and you and Mr. Damon not only saw me upon a screen in another room but also heard me?"

"Yes, both my photo telephone and my talking pictures embodied features of television."

"And it isn't saying too much that both of them were ahead of their times," Ned added.

"Yes, they were somewhat," admitted Tom with a smile. Those of you who are interested in knowing what Tom Swift accomplished with the telephone which enabled a person to see to whom he was talking, and the apparatus by which persons moving and talking in one room could be viewed by an audience some distance away, are referred to those respective volumes in this series.

"No, Ned," went on the young inventor, "I wouldn't balk at a thing because it was hard. But just now I'm so upset about the theft from my secret vault that I can't think of much else. The television detector may come in time, but just now I want to get hold of the man who took that gas formula."

"You may need a television detector to do that," Ned argued.

"I may. But first I'm going to try ordinary clues such as looking for fingerprints and other detective stuff. This surely is tough luck."

"I'm sorry about it, Tom. But it's a good thing you have discovered the theft in time. You can take precautions."

"I'm not so sure I have discovered it in time, Ned. There's no telling when the place was entered. I haven't been in it myself for several weeks. This robbery may have taken place right after my latest visit when the formula was there, or it may have happened today."

"Is there no way of telling, Tom?"

"None that I know of. I haven't any time-lock on my vault. I wish I had. I thought it was secure enough as it was, and I don't see how in the world the thieves ever got in. I'll have to make a careful examination tomorrow."

"I'll help," Ned offered. "But this thing about a secret formula for a deadly war gas is new to me."

"I know it is, Ned, and I'm going to tell you about it. It's rather a simple story. Some time ago, through one of my agents, I learned of a foreigner who had invented a deadly, poisonous gas. It was just before the World War and he intended to sell it to one of the European governments. I heard of it, and the stories telling of its almost instantaneous and deadly effect were hardly believable.

"I managed to get into communication with this foreigner. He was in this country at the time and gave me a demonstration of the gas."

"You mean he let it kill a lot of people for you, Tom?"

"Of course not! Don't be silly! We used it on

a horde of rats, and the way those rodents keeled over was enough to show me what it could do if used on humans. The result was that I bought the full rights from him, Ned. The formula became mine to do with as I pleased and this man agreed, after I paid him a large amount of money, never to disclose the secret to anyone or to use it himself in any way."

"Could you trust him, Tom? I mean, he might have sold the formula to you and later sold it to someone else."

"That possibility occurred to me, and I was trying to devise ways of protecting myself when this man died, and, I have reason to believe, before he had a chance to disclose the secret formula to anyone. It was very complicated. It wasn't a formula you could write on a small piece of paper. There were many processes involved."

"But what in the world did you want of it, Tom? You weren't going into the poison gas business, were you?"

"Not in a thousand years. I bought it to save and protect humanity. I figured that if I had the formula safe in my secret vault no one could use it, not even our own United States. It was too horrible! You should have seen those rats die!"

"I'm glad I didn't!"

"Well, I bought the gas formula, put the

papers—there were a lot of them—in a peculiar looking box this foreigner gave me. It had a secret catch and you might try for a week to open it without any result. One who didn't know the combination would have to break the box to get at the papers. I put the chest into the hiding place and only today decided that I had better take a look at the documents. I got to thinking the vault might be damp and might affect the ink. So I went down with you. You know what happened."

"The deadly gas formula is gone."

"Stolen! And I must find the man who took it or he may kill off whole countries or states if he is a fanatic. Ned, I've my work cut out for me."

"Then you won't be interested in my secret code or in making a television detector?"

"Not until I get this formula back. Hello! What's that?"

A noise was heard in the corridor outside the laboratory. Then Koku's voice was heard shouting:

"Master! Come quick! Someone try to get in! Come quick, Master!"

Tom and Ned leaped for the door outside of which came a scuffling sound and then a wild, ringing cry.

CHAPTER III

KOKU SEES A MAN

TOM SWIFT and his chum reached the corridor outside the laboratory in time to see a man leap through the outer door. It was late afternoon and the cloudy day produced, inside, a gloom that did not make for easy visibility. In a glance Tom and Ned decided that the intruder was a man they had not seen before, or at least one whom they had not seen often.

"Get him, Ned!" cried Tom. "I'll look after Koku!"

"The giant is hurt!" gasped Ned as he saw the prostrate form of the big man lying on the floor. There was wonder as well as alarm in Ned's voice, for he and Tom had regarded Koku as almost invincible. Yet he had been felled by this stranger—this unknown man who had made his way into the laboratory building while Tom and Ned were below in the secret vault making the momentous discovery of the theft of the terrible gas formula.

"Koku seems to be knocked out!" spoke Tom, bending over his big and faithful servant. "I can't see how it happened. That fellow is not much more than ordinary size, yet he knocked out a giant. See if you can catch him, Ned. But look out! Evidently he's a dangerous customer!"

"I'll be careful! I'll get help! You see to Koku!"

Ned dashed out into the yard of the plant, calling an alarm as he went. The watchman at the big gate, one of the main entrances to the Swift works, heard him and came up on the run. Ned caught a glimpse of the intruder who had fled from the laboratory leaping along, jumping over piles of lumber and discarded machinery.

"Get that man!" cried the manager to the guard and several workmen who had joined him. "He hurt Koku!"

"He must be some fellow to do that!"

The light of the fading day was fast disappearing as the chase started. Then the pursuit ended almost as quickly as it had begun. For one moment the man was in sight amid a conglomeration of material in the yard, and two seconds later he had disappeared from view. There was no outlet, at this point, in the big fence that surrounded the plant. To climb over it without a ladder was impossible and there was no sign of a ladder. Even with that help it would have been dangerous to try to pass the barrier, for it was protected by electrically-charged wires.

"I don't know whether or not the current is on now," Ned remarked to some of the men who had come up to join him in the chase.

"No, it isn't," said one. "Mr. Swift hasn't had the juice on lately as there hasn't been any trouble."

"There's been plenty of trouble this afternoon," thought Ned. "And I guess from now on we'll keep the wire charged. Let's see if we can dig this fellow out," he went on. "Scatter, men, and look for him!"

"He disappeared mighty suddenly, Mr. Newton," remarked the gate watchman. "What did he do?"

"I don't know just what he did, except to knock out Koku," was the answer, and there were murmurs of surprise at this statement. "Mr. Swift and I were discussing some private business in the laboratory a little while ago," went on Ned. "We had Koku out in the hall on guard. All at once he yelled and Mr. Swift and I rushed out to see the giant down and this man running off."

"Did he get away with anything, I mean any of Mr. Swift's papers or machines?" asked a workman.

"We don't know yet for sure," was Ned's cautious answer. The secret of the vault and the formula must be maintained at all hazards, even from Tom Swift's own men.

"He probably was trying to sneak in and steal something," was one man's comment. "It's happened before."

"Well, I don't believe he can get out of this place," said another. "Even if the fence isn't protected by the juice, it's too high to climb and all the gates are guarded."

"All except the one I just left!" exclaimed the guard as he happened to recall how suddenly he had rushed away. "I forgot to get anybody to take my place."

"That was the natural thing to do," remarked the manager. "But you'd better get right back to it, Perkfeld. We'll look for this chap."

Perkfeld hastened back to the unguarded gate while Ned and the workmen, some with powerful flashlights, began looking around for the fleeing intruder. They did not find him, but that was not surprising, for the yard at this point was cluttered up with supplies and discarded machinery.

"I'd better be getting back to Mr. Swift," Ned remarked after a few minutes of unproductive search. "You men keep on looking for this chap and if you get him——"

"We'll know what to do with him, Mr. Newton!" significantly remarked one of them with a grim chuckle.

"I guess you will," Ned answered.

He hurried back to the laboratory, where he

found that Tom and some men from the dynamo shop nearest the experiment room had carried Koku to a couch in Tom's private office. The giant seemed to be reviving under the strong whiffs of ammonia being given him. The air of the office was pungent with the odor of the stimulant.

"Did you find out anything, Tom?" Ned asked.

"Not much of value. Did you get that man?"

"No! He seems to have disappeared, but the boys are looking for him around the yard. He was a fast runner."

"He couldn't get over the fence," Tom argued. "Not without a ladder, and he didn't have one."

"Unless it was a rope one under his coat," Ned stated. "Too bad you didn't have the juice on the fence wire."

"That's so!" exclaimed the young inventor. "I'll put it on now and keep it on after what happened," and his look at Ned was significant. Quickly he went to a telephone and gave the order to the electrical department. In a few moments the Swift plant was protected by a powerful, though not deadly, current circulating through wires on top of the high fence. In addition, lights gleamed all along the lengths of the barrier. A general alarm was given that all strangers were to be excluded or apprehended as the case might be.

"Though I'm afraid it's too late," remarked Tom as he came back.

"The boys may get him," voiced Ned, referring to the fleeing intruder who had so mysteriously vanished. "But what happened to Koku?"

"That's just what we're trying to get at," Tom said. "He was completely knocked out."

"By a blow or some injury?" Ned inquired.

"No, we can't find a mark on him and he says he isn't hurt. I guess he can answer questions now. What happened, Koku?"

"Me on guard as Master tell," rumbled the giant. "Then Koku see man walk in like big cat. Koku ask him what for. Then Koku feel queer and he call and yell and then he fall down."

"Chloroformed!" exclaimed Ned.

"Or doped in some way," agreed Tom. "I shouldn't say it was chloroform, for there aren't any burns around Koku's face which a chloroformed rag would produce, and there was no odor of the drug when I got to him. But he was overcome all right, and not by physical force, either."

"What then?" asked Ned in a low voice.

"Some kind of gas," was Tom's whispered reply. "We'll talk of that later. Feel better now, Koku?"

"Yes, Master. Much better. Koku go get man

what knocked him down. Koku make him—so!"
and the giant made a motion of breaking something in his powerful hands.

"You take it easy now," Tom suggested with
a smile. "Rest up a bit. We'll look for that
stranger and if we catch him we may let you
guard him, Koku."

There was suddenly a little commotion in the
corridor outside the private office and a quaver-
ing voice was heard to say:

"Am Massa Tom in dere?"

"Oh, yes, Rad, what is it?" inquired the
young inventor as he recognized the voice of the
old Negro, Eradicate Sampson.

"Yo' Pa done sent me t' see whut was de
mattah. He say he heah some ruction in heah."

"Come in, Rad," invited Tom kindly.
"There's nothing much wrong. Just another attempt at theft. You go back and tell my father
everything is all right. Then you take Koku to
his quarters and see that he goes to bed. He
has been knocked out."

"Ho! Dat big giant knocked out!" chuckled
Eradicate, and it seemed that he received the
news with pleasure. There was always a rivalry
between the two servitors of Tom Swift. "Come
along wid me, Koku!" went on the Negro.

For once in his life the giant was content to
follow his pygmy rival, much to the delight of
Eradicater who led the way on tottering legs.

Koku was really much weakened by the effect of the gas or some knock-out poison that had been used on him.

"This is very strange, Tom," remarked Ned when they were alone in the laboratory.

"Yes, it surely is. When they get Koku they're playing dangerously near our goal line. Poor Rad!" he murmured.

"Why, he wasn't hurt, was he?" asked Ned.

"No, but I can't help noticing how old and feeble he's growing. I guess it won't be long now before he follows his mule, Boomerang, to the happy hunting grounds, or wherever it is good mules go. Poor Rad!"

"He's a faithful old soul," commented Ned. "But Tom, what's the next move in this mystery?"

"Mystery is right, Ned. I must find out who it was that got into my vault, and how. And I'll get back that formula if it's the last thing I do. That gas is more dangerous than T. N. T."

"I'll go out and see if the men have any trace of that fellow. Do you think he might be the one who took the formula?"

"I don't see how he could be. He didn't come out of the vault."

"He may have been there before to get the box containing the formula papers and this time returned to see what else he could steal."

"Maybe. Well, see if there's any news."

Ned hurried out. That a search of the yard was still going on but without result, was the news the manager brought back to Tom's office.

"Well, we can't do any more today," Tom decided. "I must think this thing out if I can. We'll make a fresh start tomorrow. Meanwhile I'll set a guard about this place."

"And I'm going to work at perfecting my secret code," declared Ned. "We may need it, Tom, sooner than you think."

"We may, Ned. Go to it! I'm going home. My wife and Dad must be anxious or they wouldn't have sent Rad to find out the news. See you in the morning."

"Right, Tom!"

Tom Swift and Ned Newton sat up late that night. The young inventor after assuring his pretty wife that he was quite unhurt, labored over the mysterious problem of who had robbed his secret vault. On his part, Ned was working out a simple but puzzling secret code with which he could communicate with Tom by means of a portable wireless set in case there should ever be need for it.

"And there may be need any time," mused Ned as he pored over his work.

As for Tom, his problem was still unsolved when he went to bed long past midnight.

There was no news the next morning. The night force had been unable to find any trace of the intruder and there had been no further disturbance at the plant. The guards around the office and laboratory had seen no intruders.

Tom and Ned met in the office about nine o'clock, and after the former had told the manager he had not thought of any solution of the problem, he added:

"We'll make an inspection of the whole plant today. There may be a leak somewhere. Ask Martin to bring up the electric runabout. We can cover a lot of ground in that and it's small enough to negotiate in narrow quarters. We'll take Koku with us."

"Koku?"

"Yes. He's all right this morning. It may be this rascal is still in hiding and if Koku should see him he'd know him."

"That's right. I'll get Martin to run the car over."

A little later the two young men and Koku were making a tour of the big manufacturing plant in Tom's electric runabout, an improved model of one in which Tom and Ned had had some surprising adventures. It was easy to handle and could make short turns.

In and out, up and down the big plant yard the three rode, Koku as much on the alert as were his companions. They were approaching the south gate, little used, which gave access to the storage section of the plant, and were swinging around a big pile of lumber, when suddenly the giant cried:

"Koku see a man!"

"What man?" asked Tom quickly.

"Man from yesterday—man what blow smoke in Koku's face! Look! Him got here!"

CHAPTER IV

A SLENDER CLUE

Speeding out from amid the lumber piles was a man—a tall, powerfully built fellow with a face, as Tom and Ned could see when he turned it partly toward them, almost covered by a black beard.

"There he go!" cried Koku.

And literally the man went. One moment he was in plain sight, the next he was gone. He had been speeding toward the fence. The south gate was not only closed but a man was on guard there as was the case at the other portals.

"We'll get him, Ned!" cried Tom as he turned more power into the electric runabout.

"But he's gone!" echoed Ned.

And gone the fellow was. He seemed to have evaporated as if he had turned into vapor or smoke.

"We must follow him!" shouted Tom.

Though the electric runabout could do many things, it could not with safety charge through a heavy wooden fence. To continue the chase, since it was evident that the man had run out

31

of the yard, the runabout must pass beyond the fence.

"How he ever got out is a mystery," Ned remarked.

"We'll soon solve it," said Tom Swift grimly.

He had to turn his car about and make for the gate, an evolution that lost him nearly a minute, for the watchman had left his keys in the gate-house while he was cultivating a small patch of tomatoes. Since the south gate was little used, he was growing the fruit to occupy his spare time. When the car finally emerged into the highway which ran along the part of the Swift property where the black-bearded intruder had disappeared, the stranger was not within sight.

"He's gone!" murmured Ned in disappointed tones.

"Maybe we can trace him," said Tom hopefully. "We'll run up and down the road a ways and make some inquiries."

This they did, but without result. They described the foreigner, for such he evidently was, to persons they met, but no one had any information. Then, giving up reluctantly, Tom and Ned, with Koku, returned to the south gate.

"No, Mr. Swift, I didn't see anything of a man with a black beard," the south gate watchman answered in response to an inquiry. "He didn't come in this way and he didn't go out this way. My gate hasn't been unlocked in nearly a week."

"Well, he got in and he got out—somehow!" declared Tom. "I'm going to inspect the fence near the place where he disappeared."

When this was done it was at once seen how entrance had been gained and how the man had been able to get out so quickly. There was a hole beneath the fence large enough for even the big body of the foreigner to slip through. That the man was a foreigner both Tom and Ned agreed, though his nationality, save that it was European or Asiatic, was not so certain.

"So he got out this way," mused Ned as he and Tom stood looking at the hole beneath the fence.

"And in this way, too, probably," agreed Tom ruefully. "That's no doubt how he made his escape yesterday, though it doesn't explain how he got into my vault."

"Wires cut and cleverly joined so as not to set off the alarm," went on Ned as he and his chum made a closer inspection of the hole. "He must be clever, all right."

"Too clever!" muttered the young inventor. "And dangerous! If he has that gas formula——" Tom Swift did not finish the sentence but Ned could guess his meaning.

It must not be supposed that Tom Swift would so carefully guard his plant with a high

fence protected on top by a wire carrying a
high voltage charge of electricity, and neglect
the ground section. Almost any fence is easily
tunneled, and knowing this the young inventor
had buried in the earth, all along the lower edge
of the barrier, a series of fine electrical wires.
The breaking of any one of these would ring
an alarm in the central guard house, at the same
time indicating what section of the fence protection had been severed.

"But there was no alarm," Ned declared, for
supervision of this department was one of his
duties. "I've checked the reports for the past
week and not a wire was cut."

"There wouldn't be an alarm the way this
fellow worked it," said Tom with a grim smile.
"Look!"

There were several wires beneath the fence,
buried at varying depths in the earth. The
lowest one was six feet down, and the others
separated from it by one foot spaces, a space
too narrow to permit the passage of a man's
body. The wires were insulated, of course, and
the cutting of any one of them would sound an
alarm. Tom figured that if anybody should try
to dig down below six feet it would be such a
major operation, and take so long, that the work
would be seen by men who made a circuit of the
fence several times a day.

"Here's what this fellow did," stated Tom,

reconstructing what he believed had happened. "He made a shallow hole beneath the fence, taking in the first two wires. If he could prevent an alarm from coming when either of those were cut he would be safe for a time. He scraped the insulation off these two wires in two places, far enough apart to permit the passage of his body through the space and also through the hole under the fence. He joined the bare places of the wires with insulated wire loops he had with him. Then he did the cutting. There was no interruption of the current flowing in the wires because it went around the loop and kept on going. The cut made no difference, or, if it did, it was such a slight and momentary interruption that it did not register on the alarm apparatus.

"So this foreigner had a safe place to crawl through the wires without breaking them and he could also get beneath the fence. And that's what he did, escaping the same way," said Tom.

"But why didn't the guard, who walks along this fence every day, see the dirt from the hole?"

"I don't believe it was the guard's fault," Tom said. "You notice there's no dirt around here, Ned."

"But how could he dig a hole without leaving a pile of dirt?"

"There probably was dirt at first when he did his digging. But he disposed of the earth as prisoners do when they're tunneling to get out. He carried it away with him and probably covered the hole with a light covering of sticks, with some grass and a scattering of dirt, so that when the guard passed, it looked like natural ground. That's only a theory, but it's possible. Anyhow, we can see how he monkeyed with the alarm wires."

"Yes, that's plain enough," agreed Ned. "Well, maybe it wasn't the guard's fault. But we'll have to do something about these wires, Tom."

"You're right. If they can be cut and joined this way our present alarm system is no good. I never figured that we'd be beset by enemies clever enough to think of this. I'll arrange a new alarm system for the bottom of the fence at once. I may have to do as I have done at the top—run a knock-out, but not deadly, current through the wires."

"I think you'd better, Tom. What are you looking for?" asked Ned, as he observed his chum carefully inspecting the earth around the hole.

"Footprints," answered the young inventor. "Don't come too close, Ned. I think I've something here."

"What's that?"

"A clearly marked footprint that shows somebody, with a strong tendency to walk by throwing or twisting out the left foot, has been here. These marks were made by none of us. Look!"

Ned saw what Tom pointed out: the marks of shoes with new rubber heels, for the holes showed plainly. The mark of the left one had a peculiar swirl where the ball of the foot came.

"It's just as if the man did a sort of pivot motion on his left foot, turning it inward as he went along. That may be a clue for us, Ned," said the young inventor.

"I hope so. We'll have to look for a big foreigner with a black beard who pivots and turns on his left foot. That ought to be easy."

"Not necessarily. He may shave off his beard. But of course if that foot-swirling act is natural he can't change it. I'm beginning to have some hope."

"You'd better get busy with that television detector of yours," Ned advised. "Can't tell when you may want it."

"I don't believe very soon, Ned, any more than you'll need that secret code to communicate with me when you're kidnapped."

"That won't be long, Tom."

"You mean you expect to be kidnapped?"

"No. But I was working on my code last night. I'll soon have it ready. Then you and I will practice."

"I don't mind doing that. Now I want to find

out what Koku meant when he said this man puffed smoke in his face."

"Yes, that was a queer statement."

Since there was nothing to be gained by remaining longer at the hole in the fence, and as they proved, by casting about, that they could not trace the peculiar footprint very far, Tom and Ned rode back with Koku to the office. Men were sent to readjust the doctored wires and fill up the hole. Orders were given to start work at once on a new type of alarm for the lower part of the fence. Then Tom and Ned had time to question the giant.

"You are sure this was the intruder, Koku?" asked Tom.

"Him same man—yes. Blow smoke—knock Koku down."

"What do you mean—smoke?" asked Tom.

Thereupon the giant explained, partly in his own language when he was puzzled for the English word, that when he approached the black-bearded man who had so suddenly appeared in the corridor, the intruder had made a motion with one hand toward Koku's face. There was something like a puff of smoke and Koku had gone down and out.

"Smoke!" murmured Ned, puzzled.

"Some sort of tear gas, I believe," Tom said. "It didn't leave any odor and it wasn't tear gas, of course, or we'd have noticed the effects of it not only on Koku but on ourselves. It must be some new kind of knock-out vapor, quick-acting, which leaves no trace or after-effects. And that fits in with the other things that happened."

"Meaning what?" asked Ned.

After Koku had been sent back to his quarters, Tom explained.

"That the man who tried to sneak into my laboratory is an expert chemist or an associate of one, and that's why he took the deadly formula from my vault. He knows how to make use of it. We must surely catch that scoundrel, Ned!"

"I agree with you. But how?"

"We'll have to go scouting around. We have a clue now, a slender one, but still a clue."

"You mean the queer foot mark?"

"Yes. By it we may be able to trace this man. I'm going to devote all my time to recovering the stolen formula."

"And to do that, Tom, you'll need that television detector. You'll see if you won't!"

"You've television detectors on the brain, Ned," Tom laughed.

"Well, maybe I have. That and my secret code."

Tom and Ned had been sitting in the private office talking over what had happened and speculating on the future. Tom Swift was plainly worried, as his face showed. Now he arose and paced about the room, as persons will when they are trying to think out a problem. Suddenly he came to a stop in front of a dial on the wall. It was like that of a thermostat and Ned saw the hand of it moving slightly.

"Look!" cried Tom suddenly. "Someone's trying to get into my secret vault again! That's the alarm going off!"

He sprang toward the picture of his father— the portrait that concealed the mechanism which controlled the flooring above the access to the vault.

CHAPTER V

THE TWISTING FOOT

Slowly the section of the floor moved into the recess prepared for it, and Tom and Ned stood on the edge of the opening leading by way of the iron stairs to the secret vault below.

"Can there be anyone down there, Tom?" asked Ned in a low voice.

"I don't see how it's possible. Yet the alarm indicates it. Look!"

He pointed to the moving hand on the dial. It was still vibrating slightly.

"We'll take no chances!" went on the young inventor in a low voice, locking the door of his office so that no one could come in and discover the secret of the vault by observing the hole in the floor. Then cautiously they went down.

Tom paused before the steel door that gave access to the vault proper. It was closed and locked.

"Listen!" cautioned Ned as Tom was about to work the mechanism.

"Did you hear something?" asked the young inventor, pausing.

"No. But I think we ought to listen before opening that door. There may be someone in the vault, Tom."

"I don't see how he could possibly get in."

"By tunneling from below, perhaps."

"Impossible!" exclaimed Tom. Yet so many strange things had happened of late that he did as Ned directed and placed his ear against the steel door. No sound came from within and when the portal was swung back no intruder was visible nor was there any sign of a disturbance.

"I wish someone had been in here," remarked Tom Swift with a grim smile as he opened the secret niche that had held the deadly formula.

"Why?" asked Ned in surprise.

"He might have brought back that foreign box containing the formula papers. But no such luck. The place is empty."

"If no one was here how did the alarm go off?" asked Ned.

"That's what I must find out," Tom answered, "and you'll have to help me. I don't want to bring anyone else down into this place. We'll have to work on the problem ourselves."

This the two young men did late that night when the plant was deserted except for the watchmen, as no night force was on duty at this particular time. Descending into the secret vault by the iron stairway, having placed Koku on guard out in the corridor, the young inventor and his chum sought the reason for the mysterious setting off of the alarm. Koku was instructed to be on the alert against anyone who, in spite of the vigilance of the watchmen, might sneak in on him.

"No make fool of me two times," said the giant with a meaning laugh. "I watch careful."

It took some little time, and not a little expert work on the part of Tom and Ned, before they found what was wrong with the vault alarm. Then they discovered where the insulation had worn off a small wire, causing a short circuit under certain circumstances. And the circumstances occurred whenever there was sufficient vibration to cause the wire to tremble enough to make a connection.

"But what caused the vibration today?" asked Ned.

"I remember now," Tom answered. "Just before the hand on the dial in my office moved one of the trucks went through the yard carrying some of the new giant magnets we're turning out for the navy. The ground trembled. Even down in this vault there must have been some vibration which jiggled the wire and set off the alarm. There was no one in here at all."

"Not now, but there was before," said Ned.

"Oh, yes," Tom quickly agreed. "There was an intruder here who stole that formula and nothing more, it seems, for I haven't missed anything else." They had made a checkup while seeking the cause of the alarm going off.

"And maybe that black-bearded foreigner, who was here to steal the formula, monkeyed with the alarm wires," Ned stated.

"Perhaps," agreed the young inventor. "That insulation has been scraped off—it isn't worn. There's nothing to wear it. Ned, I'm afraid we're up against a deep plot here."

"It looks so, Tom. But at least this was a false alarm."

"It was, but it's one of the exceptions that are falsely said to prove the rule. It means my vault isn't secure any more unless I do something about it."

"What are you going to do?"

"For one thing, as I said before, change the alarm system here and put on new locks. That ought to keep out whoever has solved the secret of my present kind of safeguards."

"And for the second thing?"

"We're going to scout around and follow up the clue of the man with the twisting left foot. I'm convinced he's somewhere in this neighborhood, hiding until he can either steal something else from me or until he can safely travel away with that deadly gas formula."

"What's to prevent him from skipping out whenever he pleases, Tom?"

"There's only one reason I can think of now. He may be working with a gang of plotters, such as some of the bands that are so common in Europe—bands of terrorists and bombers. This man may be only one of many and may have conceived the idea, all by himself, of stealing the formula of Korbis Alhazar."

"Korbis Alhazar!" repeated Ned. "Who's he?"

"The man from whom I purchased the gas formula to prevent it from falling into the hands of unscrupulous men," Tom answered. "I guess I didn't mention his name before."

"No, you didn't," said Ned. "But go on. You were forming a theory as to the reason this thief might be in hiding for a time. Why?"

"Because he may have broken with the gang of plotters and may be trying something on his own. In that case he'd want to evade them, but they may be close after him so he'd have to make a getaway as best he could. Perhaps he's being watched so closely that he can't get out of Shopton, and in that case we may pick up his trail by scouting around."

"I see. Say, Tom, it's something fierce if we have a gang of terrorists in Shopton!"

"We may have, though I don't believe they have any designs on our town."

"What, then?"

"I think they're trying to get some more of

my secrets. I must take better precautions, Ned."

The next few days were busy ones for Tom Swift and those associated with him. He and Ned, working alone, changed the alarm system in the secret vault and put on different locks. An inspection showed that no tunneling had been attempted, so it was decided that the intruder must have got in through the laboratory to steal the gas formula. The locks and fastenings, as well as the alarm wires connected with the building, were altered.

Meanwhile the fence about the Swift plant had been made more impregnable and the guards had been changed about. Some who were regarded as inefficient were dispensed with and new ones were substituted.

Then Tom and Ned started in to comb Shopton and its environs for a trace of the twisting footed foreigner. They made cautious inquiries and followed many clues. Most of these were false and led nowhere. During his spare moments Ned worked on his new secret code, and after many days perfected the machine for sending messages—a small, portable radio set. What he wanted to do was to communicate with Tom, through the ether, so that regardless of the interception of the signals he could make sense of it.

"And that wasn't easy," Ned remarked.

"I believe you," agreed Tom. "I must take time soon to try it out with you."

It was one day, about two weeks after the theft of the deadly gas formula, that Tom and Ned were out in the electric runabout, scouting in the suburbs for some possible clue to the twisting footed foreigner. They had inspected many footprints in soft ground, seemingly a hopeless task, looking toward tangible results, when at last they found what they thought they wanted.

They were near a section of the outskirts of Shopton where many foreigners lived. Some of them were laborers in Tom's plant and the locality was partly made up of what are termed "slums." There were drab and dreary tenements and several old factory buildings that had been made into barracks for groups of men who shifted about from place to place, working a few days or weeks in one plant and then moving on.

It was after a rain, and as Tom and Ned were driving in the electric car past a tumble-down, old brick barrack, they saw, plainly imprinted in the soft mud of a path leading to a side door, several footprints. Why he stopped to examine them Tom never knew, but he did. He and Ned had looked over so many without result that they had nearly given up. But at the sight of these Tom pointed and exclaimed:

"Ned! We've found him!"

"What do you mean—found him!"

"Look! The twisting foot!"

The two boys bent over the marks in the red mud.

"Yes," murmured the young manager, "there it is! The twisting foot!"

CHAPTER VI

A TELEVISION DETECTOR

ELATED by their discovery, yet almost distrusting their good luck and ever on the alert for danger, Tom and Ned paused for a moment and glanced from the footprints in the soft mud toward the brick building. It had a sinister appearance, so ruined was it, and seemed to contain much evil. That it was the abode of desperate men was well known about Shopton. More than once it had been raided by the police when the ugly tramp population had grown menacing.

"Do you think Twisting Foot is in there?" asked Ned, giving the suspected man this name on the spur of the moment.

"He headed for there, anyhow," remarked the young inventor. "We can't be sure he's inside without taking a look."

"And that's just what I don't want you to do, Tom."

"Why not?"

"It's dangerous. See those men."

As the young manager spoke, several ugly

faces could be observed, almost like threatening shadows, peering out of the windows, the glass of which was very dirty with the grime of years.

Then there came to a side door a shuffling figure—a brute of a man with arms and shoulders like those of a gorilla. His bearded face also somewhat resembled that animal.

"A tough customer!" Tom murmured.

"There's more than one like him inside there," spoke Ned in a low voice, for the "gorilla" seemed to be looking intently at the two young men and the sporty car. Doubtless he wondered, as did others in the barracks which might contain Twisting Foot, what the boys wanted. But the dwellers in this ruin were too familiar with the visits of the police to resent such a casual inspection as now was being given them. They may have thought Tom and Ned were building inspectors.

"Yes, maybe it wouldn't be advisable to go inside," agreed Tom. "But I should like to know whether or not that foreigner, who has at least twice visited me, is in there. And I'd like to inspect the room where he stays. I might get back that formula."

"Dangerous, Tom! Dangerous!" warned Ned.

"I believe you!"

"You might get police help," suggested the young manager.

"That's just what I don't want to do," Tom responded. "As soon as I call in the police I'll have to explain my reason for wanting to see this Twisting Foot. Then the story of the deadly gas formula would come out and there would be a lot of trouble. I'll have to work in secret and try to locate this man. In some way, though it isn't clear to me just how I can do it, I must force him to give up that box. If we were only sure he is in there now!" and Tom looked longingly at the building and then at the tell-tale footprints.

"There's only one way to find out without actually going inside, which would be dangerous," Ned stated.

"I know," Tom was quick to reply, for his brain worked ever faster than Ned's. "Your old scheme of a portable television detector."

"That's it! You're the only one who can get that machine up in a hurry and this is the time to use it. I don't mean you can rush back to your laboratory and make a television detector in half an hour, but you have the groundwork now and it ought not to take long."

"Making a portable one isn't so easy," Tom said. "But at that, Ned, I think your advice is good. The trouble is that by the time I get the detector to working, providing I can, this Twisting Foot may have skipped out."

"You said he would probably hang around

here for a while, afraid to leave," suggested Ned.

"Yes, he may. But there's no telling how long."

"Well, he has such prominent characteristics, the twisting foot especially, that he ought to be easy to trace. I should think the police here could help. You wouldn't have to give away the secret of the gas formula, by just asking some officers to come here and find out from some of the characters who hang out here where Twisting Foot has gone—if he goes."

"Yes, I suppose I could do that, Ned."

"Then do it! Get busy on the television detector, bring it here in a car and get an X-ray cross-section of the interior of that old factory. You may see Twisting Foot in one of the dens there, trying to solve the secret of the formula."

"Golly, Ned! I believe you're right and I'll do it!" exclaimed Tom Swift with more enthusiasm than he had shown in a long while. "Yes, I'll see if I can make a television detector that will enable me to look through a brick wall. Let's go!"

The two young men departed in the electric runabout, probably to the relief of the inhabitants of the old, ruined building. Whether or not the character designated as Twisting Foot was among them neither Tom nor Ned had any means, then, of knowing.

It was characteristic of Tom Swift that, once

he started anything, he worked feverishly at it until he had achieved success. On his return to the laboratory with Ned, the young inventor sent to the storehouse for two of his formerly successful machines. One of these was the photo telephone, a device that could be attached to the talking and receiving apparatus so that two persons in conversation could see images, one of the other, on a metallic-glass plate.

"This wouldn't do for what we have in mind," Tom said to his chum as they tried out the machine. "To use this we need coöperation at both ends. In the television detector I want to be the only one to use the apparatus and it must be without the knowledge of the other party."

"That's right," Ned agreed.

"But there are parts of this gadget I can use, I think," said Tom, looking it over carefully. "Now where's the first model I made for my talking picture machine?"

"Here," Ned answered when a workman had brought it in.

"Let's give this a trial," Tom suggested. "I'll set up the transmitting part in that little room down the hall and you can do some stuff, Ned. I'll see how I get it here. Distance is only relative, anyhow. I know one thing I'll have to do, though."

"What's that?" asked Ned as Tom went to a steel safe where he kept supplies.

"I must use a new style of tube, some of which I have on hand. The old cathode tubes won't answer now, especially if I make a portable television detector. I'll need a lot of power in a small space."

"Can you get it?" asked Ned anxiously.

"Yes. What I plan on using in this new television is a double anode, high vacuum, cathode ray oscillograph tube and——"

"That's enough!" interrupted Ned with a laugh. "I'll let you attend to the technical end of it. All I'm interested in is results. But I'll act my stuff for you and you can see how the old machine works."

"I'll try it first with the old tubes," Tom decided, "and then put in new ones."

"With a name as lengthy as my arm," chuckled Ned. "Go to it!"

It did not take long to set up the apparatus which was in simple, model form. By inventing it and selling the manufacturing rights to a concern some years before, Tom Swift had made considerable money.

Ned, as he had done when Tom first tried out his talking-moving picture apparatus, went into a far room, took his place near the transmitting device and began to sing and dance. He was not at all worried about the quality of his performance. He just wanted to help Tom. He rattled off a popular song, did a few steps, and then went to an inter-communicating telephone to find out from Tom how the reception had been.

"As good as it was before, Ned," Tom answered. "But try it again in a little while. I'm going to use the new tubes with the long name you object to. I'll give you the signal by the buzzer when I'm ready."

In a short time the buzzer sounded and again Ned did his song and dance. In his laboratory Tom Swift was looking at a metallic screen, impregnated with mysterious electrical waves coming from new and high-powered tubes with double anodes and high vacuum exhaustion. The first image of Ned had been rather faint. Now the somewhat shadowy figure of the young manager greatly brightened and became sharp and clear on the screen. His voice, too, as he sang, grew louder.

"That's fine, Ned!" Tom Swift reported over the inside telephone. "I think I'm on the right track. The new tubes will solve the problem. Come on back."

Presently the two were together again.

"How soon can you make the television detector, Tom?" asked his chum.

"It isn't as easy as you think," Tom answered. "What we have just used was a sort of double apparatus. I must devise a single one that will enable me to see through a building and observe the inmates who don't know they are being looked at. I'll have to generate in my own portable machine not only the power by which I see but also the power that will enter the building and transmit the images. No, it isn't going to be easy. But I'll do it!"

"I'm sure you will, Tom. I'll help all I can and——"

"Hark!" interrupted the young inventor. "Someone is coming!"

Footsteps sounded in the corridor outside the laboratory. As it was late at night and as orders had been given that he was not to be disturbed, Tom felt that the presence of an intruder might mean danger.

CHAPTER VII

THE LEOPARD'S SPOTS

SILENT and alert, the two waited in the laboratory as the footsteps came nearer and nearer. Tom was wondering how anyone had got past Koku, who was on guard, when suddenly a voice exclaimed:

"Bless my potato salad! You don't need to come with me to show me the way, Koku! I've been here before!"

"Mr. Damon!" murmured Ned with a laugh.

With rather a foolish grin on his face, Tom Swift opened the door. A moment later the eccentric man who had taken part in so many of Tom's adventures entered the room.

"Ah, there you are!" he almost shouted in his joy at again seeing the two friends, for he had not visited them in some months. "I'm just in time, I hope."

"Time for what?" Tom asked.

"Bless my excursion ticket, in time for another adventure, I hope, Tom. This looks like it!" and he pointed toward the various pieces of apparatus scattered about the room.

"This is old stuff, Mr. Damon," Ned remarked. "You remember the photo telephone and the picture transmitter, don't you?"

"Sure I do! Bless my shoe laces but those were great days! But aren't you going somewhere or going to do something, Tom?"

"Why do you ask?" inquired the young inventor.

"Because if you are going on a trip I want to go with you," was the answer. "My wife has gone to visit her mother. I'm at a loose end, Tom, and if you are going off in a submarine or up in your sky train or the big dirigible, why I'm with you. In other words, I am on my vacation and I want to have some fun."

"Sorry, but I'm not planning any trips," Tom replied. "I've a lot of work to do here, Mr. Damon."

"That's too bad. Well, then I won't bother you. But I'll drop in again. You may change your mind. I just saw my wife off on the midnight train, and wanting something to do I decided to come here even if it was late. I saw lights in the laboratory and Koku let me in. I hope I didn't disturb you, Tom."

"Not at all. Ned and I had finished experimenting for the time. But I don't contemplate any trips."

"Then I'll have to go on one myself, maybe just a short one," said the odd man. "Bless my cheese cake, but I must do something now that my wife is away. Well, I'll see you again," and he went out, blessing his hat for Koku on the way.

"Queer character," murmured Tom as he put away the valuable television tubes in the safe.

"But jolly to have along on a trip," added Ned. "As for going away, Tom, you may have to trail this Twisting Foot chap after you get the television detector working."

"I may, Ned. We'll cross that bridge when we come to it. And now I'm going to bed."

"Same with me," murmured the young manager.

Early the next day Tom Swift resumed experimental work on the new apparatus which he hoped would not only aid him in discovering the thief who had taken the formula, but which might also be of practical advantage along similar lines for police and government authorities.

"Lots of times," mused Tom as he worked out formulae for various different television tubes, "the authorities would like to know if a certain man is in a certain place. The only way they can find out now is by going in and seeing him, and that may prove to be dangerous if he is armed. Or some stool-pigeon may tell the police. If I can get this jigger to work all that the authorities would need to do would be to point the receiver at the building or suspected hiding place, turn on the power, and they could see, on a television screen, whether or not the man they want is there. That is, they can if I can perfect this," Tom told himself with rather a grim smile.

He worked hard all that day, being visited by neither Ned nor Mr. Damon. Where the latter was Tom did not know but Ned was busy over the company's books. That night the two friends were together in the laboratory, Ned ready to make a report to Tom on some business affairs. When this was out of the way the manager asked:

"How you coming on with the television detector?"

"Slow, Ned. Slow. But I'm getting there. I may have something to show you in about a week. And now I'm going out."

"Where?" asked Ned in some surprise.

"To that old building where we got a trace of Twisting Foot. Oh, I'm not going in or anything like that, especially not at night," Tom hastened to say. "But we haven't been there since we got that first clue and I sort of thought I'd like to look the place over again. We might happen to see that foreigner going in or out."

"Not a bad idea, Tom," Ned agreed. "I'll go with you."

They used the electric runabout to ride to

the site of the grim, ruined building, as that car made little noise and they did not want to advertise their presence. They were not long in reaching the place, which, save for a few dim lights here and there, was in sinister darkness as befitted the deeds that were no doubt being planned there.

Parking in a secluded place, Tom and Ned approached the building cautiously afoot, keeping as much as possible in the shadows. From the old shack came, now and then, bursts of laughter or rough songs.

"They're trying to imagine they're having a good time, I suppose," murmured Ned.

"Yes," Tom assented. "Poor chaps. I feel sorry for some of them. I wish I knew, though, whether or not the man who stole my formula is in there."

"You'll soon find out, Tom, when you get that detector perfected."

"I'm going to hurry work on it. This fellow, or some of those in league with him, may spring this poison gas any time. The results of using it would be terrifying!"

"All the more reason for haste then, Tom. But if they were going to use it why haven't they done so already?"

"My theory is, Ned, that they don't intend to use it here. I think this foreigner is one of a gang who may be going to let loose what would be a scourge over Europe. There is great and terrible unrest in some of those countries. The right or wrong of it all I know nothing about. But there are desperate plotters over on the other side."

"I believe you, Tom. But what can we do?"

"Get back that formula, for one thing. That will save a lot of lives. It may be there is some scheme to use it here in the United States. Some of the plotters abroad would be only too glad to see our country thrown into chaos."

"No doubt. Well, we don't seem to have started up anything here."

"I guess there isn't much use in hanging around. The chaps in there are night birds. I guess they don't even leave their nest until after midnight and they get back at dawn. Twisting Foot seems to be keeping under cover."

"He isn't in sight, anyhow," agreed Ned as they turned to go back to the runabout. "It would be pretty hard to spot him in this darkness even if he were around."

"Probably. Well, I'll have matters more my own way when I get my television machine in shape."

As Ned lived some distance from Tom's house, which was reached first on the way back, the young inventor told his chum to use the runabout in going home and to come to work in it the next day.

As Tom got out in front of his own house,

near an electric light, Ned slid over to take the wheel, and observed Tom looking at something on the side of the car.

"What is it?" Ned asked.

"Some boys must have been playing around the car when we were scouting around the old barracks," Tom answered. "They've drawn some sort of a picture on the door with mud, I guess. Look!"

Ned got out in order to see better. In the gleam of the street light he and Tom saw, drawn in dried mud or soft chalk on one of the doors, the crude representation of some animal.

"What is it?" asked Ned, laughing.

"Looks as if it were meant for a leopard."

The picture was, indeed, that of some spotted beast. To make sure there could be no mistake someone had printed beneath it the words, "spotted leopard."

"Here's a rag, wipe it off," spoke Ned, reaching into an inner door pocket and taking out a cloth.

"No!" exclaimed Tom. "Wait a minute. Here's something else!"

He pointed to some words below the picture. They were somewhat in the shadow and had not been observed as quickly as the others. As the boys looked and read, Ned gave a whistle, and Tom gasped. The words were:

"Beware the Leopard League, Tom Swift."

CHAPTER VIII

THE SECRET CODE

SILENTLY the two looked at the crude picture and the sinister warning beneath it. Then Ned laughed as he remarked:

"Nervy kids, marking up the car like that!"

Tom Swift did not reply for the moment. He stood staring at the defacement.

"Aren't they?" demanded Ned, not quite able to fathom Tom's silence.

"I don't believe boys had anything to do with this, Ned," said the young inventor, and his voice was rather solemn. "Look, these spots on the leopard are made with an impressed thumb, and from the size of it you can see it isn't a boy's."

"That's right, Tom."

"The letters in the message, too, aren't such as boys would make," went on Tom. "They show a practiced hand."

"Then what do you think, Tom, if this isn't a joke?"

"It's far from a joke, I'm afraid."

"What do you mean?"

"I mean that while we were out of the car, scouting around that old shack, Twisting Foot, or some companion of his sneaked out and left this warning."

"You regard it as a warning?"

"What else is it?"

"The Leopard League," Ned murmured. "Sounds dangerous enough. But how did they guess it was your car, Tom?"

"I don't know. How did someone get into my secret vault? I don't know that, either. But it's plain that we're on the track of some man, or band of men, to judge by the use of the words 'Leopard League'—men who don't want to be trailed or discovered. This is a warning to lay off."

"And are you going to, Tom?"

"I am not! I'll fight them now! This is growing more complicated. I begin to see, that the theft of that formula was no simple robbery on the part of a man who might want to demand a large sum from me for returning it. I believe there's a deep plot here, Ned! I'm going to fight these fellows!"

"And I'll help you! Now I'll just wipe this off, run home to get some sleep, and then——"

"Stop!" cried Tom, catching Ned's hand as he was about to use the rag to efface the picture and words on the car door. "Let it stay."

"What for?"

"I'm going to photograph it in the morning. Run the electric car into the garage and take the little gasoline roadster. This may give us a new clue."

The electric runabout was put into the Swift garage, care being taken not to obliterate any of the markings. Then Tom wrote a notice and fastened it on the machine to the effect that no one was to disturb it. Ned jumped into the gasoline roadster and he and Tom parted, each more worried over what had occurred than either of them cared to admit.

The next day Tom took photographs of the crude drawings and thumb marks on his car. The thumb marks were made up into separate photographs and Tom planned to submit them to a police finger-print expert when he could get the opportunity. Just now he decided to keep the whole thing a secret.

"It's evident," he said to Ned later when they were in his office, "that they know, or fear, I am on their trail. Not that I'm so terrible, but they don't want anyone following them. It argues guilt, Ned."

"I think so myself. Well, we're on our way to catch them. How's the television jigger coming on?"

"Not so well! I've struck several snags. But I may be able soon to snake them out and get into a clear field. It's all right in theory but the practice is where it's hard. What have you there?" he asked his chum, who had a brief-case filled with papers which he laid on a desk in the laboratory.

"Working out my secret code," Ned answered. "I've a notion, Tom, that I may have a use for this sooner than I expected. If the Leopard League catches you or me we can communicate by means of this."

"We may be able to if you get it so it can be worked and have the machine for sending it out."

"That's where I want your help, Tom. The machine I have is too big and clumsy. Can't you make one that can be carried in a fellow's pocket?"

"I might be able to. In fact, I'm sure I can. I think I'll work on that for a while and lay this television detector aside. Sometimes if I change the trend of my thoughts, I get better results when I go back to the place where I'm stuck. You work out a secret message and I'll give you the sending and receiving machines combined into one."

"That's great, Tom!"

The next week was a busy one in the Swift laboratory. Tom, laying aside for the time the problem of the new television apparatus, labored over a small machine that could be operated by carrying a tiny dry cell or by plugging it into an incandescent electric light socket. It was a combined sending and receiving radio which could transmit, by means of dots, dashes and spaces a message by the Morse code. Ned hoped Tom could make it work by the voice, but that was a little too much to expect.

"Anyhow," the youthful manager remarked when Tom had turned out two complete units which could be stowed away in a coat pocket, and which looked not unlike rather large cigarette cases, "we can signal each other when we're separated, and no one can catch on to what we say."

"That's right," Tom agreed. "Over a limited distance, of course. This won't work over a distance of more than ten miles."

"That may be far enough," Ned stated.

"But where's your code?" Tom asked. "I must learn it, you know, or it won't be of any use. We must get at it soon."

So the days went on. Tom went back to his television apparatus, Ned worked on the machine with his secret code, and once or twice the two paid a flying visit to the old barracks. They did not go at night, however, and not once did they get out of the car. They saw no further signs of Twisting Foot and there seemed to be no special activities around the abode of the derelict men.

Besides working on his new apparatus, Tom

tried, at odd times, to find out how his secret vault had been entered. There had been no other unauthorized visits to the place, but the puzzle as to how the gas formula had been taken out, in the strange box which enclosed it, remained as deep as ever.

One afternoon, when he had been busy on the problems of making a television detector that could be installed in an automobile, Ned, who was poring over several sheets of paper at his desk, remarked:

"Well, there it is!"

"What?" asked Tom with something of a start, showing his nerves to be on edge.

"My secret code," answered the young manager. "I think it's time you learn it, Tom, and we'll give it a trial."

"Can't we try it now? I mean, if you give me a copy of the code I may be able to catch your message and translate it. Later I'll get the system so fixed in my mind that I won't need any paper to look at. Let's have a go at it. I'm stuck on this television gadget and I want something to relax me."

"All right. I'll go over to the storage yard. That's about the farthest point away from the laboratory here, and I'll send you a message. I'll leave you a copy of the code so all you'll have to do will be to put down the words as I send them to you and look up the decoding formula on these papers. It'll take you longer than when you have it by heart, but that won't matter now. It's a very secret but simple code and easy to learn once you get onto the system. But it may take you a little time when you have to look it up on the papers and verify the words."

"All right, Ned, I've some leisure just at the present moment. I'll be listening for you."

Ned took the little pocket sending and receiving apparatus with him and started for the storage yard where, amid the piles of lumber, he and Tom had lost sight of the intruder that day when he escaped beneath the fence. It was nearly a half mile away from the laboratory, so big was the Swift plant.

Tom remained at his desk with a set, which was the duplicate of the one Ned had, in front of him. It would be some little time before Ned could reach the lumber yard where, as arranged, he was to pretend to be a kidnapped captive and to signal to Tom for help.

"This is a queer business," mused the young inventor as he thought of his looted vault. "How did anyone ever solve that secret? And who has that poison gas formula?"

His musings were interrupted by footsteps in the corridor outside the laboratory, and then a well-remembered voice said:

"Bless my fountain pen, Koku, you needn't

trouble to come with me! I know my way all right. Oh, how are you, Tom?" The door opened to disclose Mr. Damon.

"All right," was the answer. "Come in and sit down. I'm waiting for a message."

"A message, Tom? I hope it's from some distant place that you'll have to go to and I can go with you. My wife is still at her mother's, you see."

"It isn't that kind of a message, Mr. Damon. It's from Ned."

"Oh, is Ned away?"

"Not any farther than the lumber yard."

"But why does he have to send a message from there?"

"It's an experiment, Mr. Damon."

"Oh, an experiment. I see! Like the time I experimented with the motor cycle and it climbed a tree with me. Bless my accident insurance policy, Tom Swift, that was the first time I met you!"

"I think it was, Mr. Damon."

"We've had some stirring times since then, Tom. I wish we could have some more. I'll never get another chance like this, with my wife visiting her mother for a month. Can't you get up some sort of a trip, like the one when we captured Koku from among the giants?"

"I'm afraid not now, Mr. Damon. Later, perhaps. Sit down a moment. Ned will be radioing to me soon and I want to see if I can translate his secret code."

The two talked for a time in generalities, then suddenly the receiver on Tom's desk began to buzz, click and splutter. Soon it settled into a regular rhythm of sound and Tom realized that Ned had accomplished what he had set out to do. He was communicating with the young inventor by means of a secret code. Heard by a person who knew nothing of the system, only a jargon of words seemed to come through the ether. But by referring to the paper before him Tom was able to translate the message which was, for the moment, of no importance. Ned was just sending such sentences as:

"The weather is good here. Having a fine time. Wish you were with me. How are you?"

To these Tom replied in like manner. With the exception of the fact that he was a bit slow in translating the code, a defect which he would remedy as soon as he had studied it a little more, everything went along smoothly.

The code messages suddenly ended. There was a silence, and then, like a flash, there came to Tom, still by means of the secret words, this plea:

"Help, Tom. Quick! He's coming after me. The Leopard!"

The clicking, buzzing and sizzling suddenly ceased.

CHAPTER IX

UNKNOWN TERROR

Tom Swift did not know what to do or think for a moment. He was mentally stunned. One instant the young inventor thought the ominous words were just a little test on the part of Ned in the distant lumberyard. Then he realized, and felt sure, there was a sinister meaning in the code message. Ned would not have referred to the "leopard," otherwise.

"I believe he really is in trouble!" Tom exclaimed.

"Who?" asked Mr. Damon, who had been reading a paper during the test.

"Ned! Come on, Mr. Damon! We must save him from the leopard!"

"The leopard, Tom!" exclaimed the eccentric man. "Why, there are no wild animals around here."

"This is more than a wild animal. It's a wild man and Ned is in danger! Come on!"

Tom rushed from the laboratory, calling to Koku who was in the corridor.

"Bless my moving picture! This looks like an

adventure—some excitement!" gasped Mr. Damon as he followed Tom and the giant.

Not pausing to summon other help from among his men, Tom speeded toward the distant part of the works where, amid piles of lumber and other supplies, Ned had elected to stage his test of the secret code. It was a cluttered up place, containing many piles of raw materials, and for a few seconds after reaching it Tom and his friends were at a loss how to locate Ned. He had not specified any particular place where he would station himself to send out the signals in code, and it had not been thought necessary to do this. Neither Tom nor his chum dreamed of danger that could menace them when they were safe behind the barrier of the electrically protected fence.

"Where is he?" demanded Mr. Damon, who was running about with Tom and Koku looking amid the piles of material for a sight of the young manager. "Where is Ned?"

"That's just what I'd like to know," Tom replied, anxiety in his voice. "It looks as though Twisting Foot had him."

"Who is Twisting Foot?" asked Mr. Damon.

"I think he's the same foreigner who calls himself the Leopard," Tom answered. "Koku!" he suddenly exclaimed, "that man who made you eat the smoke," for this description best fitted, in the giant's mind, the man who had attacked him the time it was discovered Tom's secret vault had been robbed.

"Koku get him!" snarled the big man, and he began to run here and there amid the stacks of lumber which were separated by narrow passage lanes.

The search was now intensive. Tom and his friends called Ned's name but received no answer, and the young inventor was about to sound a general alarm and call all his shop force to aid in the search when, from behind a distant pile of lumber, came Koku's voice shouting:

"Me find him! Koku got!"

"Do you mean that foreigner?" asked Tom as he speeded toward the point whence came the giant's voice.

"Master Ned!" was the answer.

"Bless my pancakes!" gasped Mr. Damon. "This is exciting!" and he ran along with Tom.

They found Ned, with an ugly bruise on his forehead, lying in a pile of weeds near the high fence. The young manager seemed just recovering consciousness and beside him was the battered and broken little wireless set over which he had sent the code signal for help.

"Ned! Ned! What happened?" cried Tom, bending over his chum.

"Oh, you—you're here," Ned murmured in a weak voice. "But I guess—I guess he got away."

"Never mind about him, Ned. Are you hurt?"

"Well, not as much as I thought I was at first," and the young man's voice was stronger as his faculties returned. "He hit me a clip on the head when he couldn't get the sending set away from me and that's all I know. Maybe he gave me a whiff of that same stuff that knocked Koku out. Oh, I feel pretty rotten!"

"Too bad, Ned! But who was it?" asked Tom.

"It was the Leopard, Tom, I'm sure of that. Wait a minute until I get a drink." Koku had run to a fire hydrant, one of several in the yard, and with a flip of his hand broke the chain which held a tin cup to the water plug. Koku brought Ned a drink, which helped to revive him.

"There's no use chasing him, Tom," said the young manager as he sat up, obviously feeling much better.

"Why not?" Tom demanded.

"He got clean away!"

"How?" asked the young inventor.

"I imagine the same way he came in, flying over the fence."

"Flying over the fence, Ned? You must be——" Tom was going to say "crazy" or "dreaming," but he did not want to use those words in his chum's present condition. So he went on with: "I don't see how that's possible. Someone might get over with a ladder, but that would be dangerous with the charged wires on top. But to fly over——"

"That's just what he did, Tom. Came flying right over. I didn't see him go back, but he must have left the same way after he wrecked me. Gee, look what he did to the sender." Ruefully Ned indicated the little portable wireless apparatus.

"Never mind about that," responded Tom. "I can easily make another or repair that one. But tell me what happened. You say this Leopard came flying over the fence. Do you mean in a small plane?"

"No, he just came sailing over as if he'd dropped out of a parachute. It was one of the most surprising things I ever saw. Here's what happened. You got my code messages all right, didn't you?" Ned asked, while Mr. Damon sat down on a pile of boards to listen and Koku wandered around looking for the man who had made him "eat smoke."

"Yes, everything was going along nicely," Tom answered, "and then came the code words that I translated into your appeal for help, as the Leopard was coming at you. How did you know he was the Leopard?"

"Because of the spots, Tom. The same sort of spots that were left on your car."

"A spotted man, Ned?" Tom's voice was incredulous.

"Not exactly a spotted man, Tom," Ned replied, "but one who had some sort of a badge, or jigger, on his chest. It was a symbol of a spotted leopard, like the one on your car."

"This certainly is getting complicated," murmured Tom. "There must be a sort of Leopard League, though I didn't believe it even after I saw what was on my car. Go on, Ned."

"Well, there isn't much to tell," resumed the young manager. "I was clicking away to you, Tom, when all of a sudden this Leopard, as I call him, came flying over the fence. It was just as if he had jumped over."

"No man could jump over a fence fifteen feet high with a charged wire on top of it."

"I'm not saying he did jump over it, Tom. But it looked so and he got over the fence some way, for he landed in that soft ground over there," and Ned pointed to where lay the remains of a sand pile. "Then he came running at me and I just had time to send that message to you when he made some sort of a motion toward me and grabbed for the sending set. I held onto it, and then he hit me a clip and that's all I remember until you came just now."

Tom shook his head in bewilderment. Mr. Damon arose and went to look at what was left of the sand pile.

"Somebody did come down here, Tom," said the odd man. "Landed with both feet, and one shoe makes a different mark from the other."

Tom ran to make an observation.

"Twisting Foot!" he murmured as he saw the imprint. "Yes, it's the Leopard all right."

"An ugly customer, from all accounts," remarked Mr. Damon.

"A terror!" Ned agreed.

"An unknown terror," supplemented Tom. "How are we going to guard ourselves against an enemy who can fly over fences? Ned, I want to believe you but it seems mighty strange."

"I know it does, Tom. But I'm telling you only what happened. The Leopard just dropped right down here."

Tom looked at the high barrier again and shook his head. Then Mr. Damon said:

"Couldn't he have dropped out of an airplane?"

"Not without a parachute," Tom replied, "and there's no sign of one around here. Besides, a parachute isn't reversible. He could not jump back over the fence with it."

They all agreed to this.

The more they talked it over and the more Ned explained, the deeper the mystery and terror seemed to grow. That there was a terror in not knowing when this Leopard enemy was going to strike next both Ned and Tom agreed when, a little later, they were again in the laboratory discussing the happening. Mr. Damon was with them. Koku and some of the workmen had been sent to make a search of the plant and yard for any trace of the sinister intruder, but there was not much chance that he would be found in hiding.

"He must have gone back over the fence the same way he came in, Tom," declared Ned.

"It's a puzzle," agreed the young inventor. "If this Leopard is the fellow who stole my gas formula he's a more dangerous character than I had any idea of."

"A regular fiend," agreed Ned. "And he isn't alone, either."

"Why, I thought you said there was only one man who attacked you, Ned," remarked Mr. Damon.

"He means that this man seems to be the head of an organization that is called the Leopard League," Tom replied, and told, more in detail than before, what had occurred the night he and Ned had gone out in the electric runabout.

"It does sound rather sinister and terrorizing," agreed the eccentric man. "But what are you going to do, Tom Swift?"

"For one thing, he's going to work night and day until he perfects his television detector, aren't you, Tom?" asked Ned.

"Yes," assented the young inventor. "There's more reason than ever now for finding this Leopard. If he's going to fly over my barrier fence and make attacks in this way it's time I got more busy than I have been."

"Not that you haven't been working," Ned made haste to say, "but things are getting desperate, Tom. It looks as if this Leopard wanted to destroy the sending set so I couldn't communicate with you."

"Maybe he's an insane man," suggested Mr. Damon.

"He's tricky enough to be that," Tom agreed. "I'd like to know how he discovered the secret of——" He was going to say "vault" but changed it to "secret of getting over my high fence."

"He can fly," suggested Ned, but he smiled as he said it. He was as much puzzled as was his chum. "We must be prepared for almost anything after this. Tom, please get my sending set repaired and then you and I must practice the secret code until we get it down to perfection. And you hurry and finish the television detector."

"I will!" Tom promised. "This is the boldest challenge I've ever received. If this Leopard League gets the best of me, the Swift concern had better go out of business."

"Bless my cash book, Tom! Don't say that!" begged Mr. Damon. "Go up against these terrorists and beat them!"

"I will!" declared the young inventor.

Intensive work was now the order of the day for Tom and Ned. The manager soon recovered from the attack of the Leopard and each day he and Tom practiced the sending and receiving of the secret code until they could snap out messages without the aid of the written words in front of them.

In the intervals of this Tom worked on his television detector. At one time he would be on the verge of success and at another in despair, for failure stared him in the face. Yet he never once gave up.

Extra precautions were taken at and around the Swift plant to keep out intruders. The current both above and below the fence was increased in intensity and warning signs were put up. The guards at the gate were cautioned to be on the alert.

When they rested from their labors, which was not often, Tom and Ned made short excursions by auto in and about Shopton, looking for the Leopard's trail, but they did not pick it up. They visited the old barracks, and in hiding watched the place, but did not see Twisting Foot. Tom made guarded inquiries of the police as to the inmates of the old brick factory, but received no trace of any man who walked with a peculiar gait.

"It looks as if he had skipped," Ned remarked after one of these trailing excursions. The boys were back in the laboratory.

"Not much trace of him," admitted Tom.

"But I'm on tenter-hooks for fear I'll read in the paper, some morning, that a lot of people have been killed in a mysterious way."

"What do you mean?"

"Well, the Leopard has that gas formula. It may take him, or those in league with him, some time to combine properly the chemicals called for, but eventually they probably will do so. Then they'll begin to experiment and they may not confine their testing of the gas to rats, as Alhazar did. They'll try it on humans!"

"Beasts!" muttered Ned. "We must beat them, Tom!"

"We will, too!"

"I thought you said the formula was in a box that no one could open."

"I doubt if many could solve the secret of opening it. But there's nothing to prevent them from smashing it. Yes, there's just one thing, now that I recall it."

"What?" asked Ned, leaning back in his chair.

"There's an inscription on the box, in Latin, to this effect: 'Who destroys me destroys himself.' That may prevent them from smashing the trick box."

"What does the inscription mean?" asked Ned.

"Korbis Alhazar, who made the container to hold his deadly gas formula, told me he put the inscription there more as a bluff than anything else. Nothing really would happen if the box were to be broken instead of being opened by pressing the hidden catch. But the old man thought thus to preserve his secret a little longer by intimidating anyone who might steal the chest. The inscription in Latin could easily be read by scientists. And a scientist is the only one who would know how to make use of the formula.

"Consequently, if some unauthorized person should get possession of the box containing the formula and read the inscription he might be deterred from smashing it to get at what was within. He might imagine there was a bomb inside, or that if he destroyed the box he would ruin its contents. As I said, it was pure bluff, but it may work and this Leopard may not be able to make use of the gas formula before we nab him."

"Which I hope will be soon," murmured Ned. "But can't he solve the secret of the box, Tom?"

"If he does he's a good one. I don't say it can't be worked out by the trial and error method. But I tried it four days and then had to give up. Alhazar finally showed me."

"So that's some protection," Ned agreed. "Well, we'll hope for the best. Now that we have the secret code perfected, Tom, all we want is your television detector and we'll catch the Leopard."

"I hope so, Ned. Now we've done enough for tonight. Let's call it a day and go home."

To this the young manager agreed. He and Tom were just leaving the laboratory and Tom was calling to Koku, who had been put on guard, that his duties were over for the night, when something on the wall of the corridor opposite the door attracted the attention of the two young men.

"Look!" murmured Ned, pointing.

"The Leopard's spots again!" gasped Tom Swift.

CHAPTER X

TOM'S WILD DANCE

THEY could hardly believe their eyes, but they must. For a second look plainly showed to Tom and Ned the imprint of several yellow smears on the wall of the corridor opposite the laboratory door.

"The Leopard's spots!" murmured Tom again. "How did they get there?"

"And where is Koku?" asked Ned.

This last question was more easily answered. The giant was found sitting in his usual place when on guard, in a big chair near the entrance to the corridor leading to the laboratory. But it was evident from the drowsy eyes of the giant that he had either been dozing or had been momentarily overcome by the same mysterious "smoke" which had knocked him out before.

"Koku, has anyone been in here?" asked Tom sharply, rousing the giant.

"In here, Master? No! Nobody get past Koku."

"Someone got past him to make those spots," murmured Ned.

86

"Are you sure, Koku?" went on Tom. "Did you see the big man with the black whiskers— the 'smoke' man?"

"No come in here, Master. Koku never move."

The two young men looked at each other. Doubtless Koku was telling the truth. Certainly he had seen no one or he would have yelled an alarm before the intruder could have knocked him out by the strange vapor.

"All right," Tom said after a pause. "Go to bed now, Koku. We're through for the night."

With a yawning sigh of relief the giant went to his own quarters, leaving Tom and Ned alone in the laboratory. There were the usual watchmen outside, however, some of them making their patrol rounds.

"What happened, Tom?" asked Ned as Koku went out.

"I don't know, but we'll have a look around."

Tom took from his desk two automatics, and thus armed he and Ned made a tour of the laboratory, on the alert with ready weapons. They knew they could summon help at a moment's notice, but there was no need, for they found no intruder nor had the secret vault been entered again. Silk threads had been strung across the steel door after the new locks had been installed, and not even Tom could enter the place without breaking these strands which were renewed after each opening.

The threads were intact, proving that the vault had not been invaded since the secret formula had been stolen. Going up to the main floor again, Tom and Ned, with flashlights, made a careful inspection of the yellow smears on the wall.

"Thumb prints again," Tom murmured. "I'll photograph them and compare them with the marks on my car."

This was done at once, for Tom had the necessary camera in his laboratory. Then the marks were effaced, for the young inventor did not want any of his men to see them and remark about them. Koku had not observed them for he was on guard farther down the corridor.

"What do you think happened, Tom?" asked Ned when they were ready to lock up and go home, the laboratory watchman having been summoned for his usual nightly tour of duty. He had been allowed time off while Ned and Tom, with Koku, were in the place.

"I think the Leopard must have slipped past my giant while he was asleep and left his trademark," Tom said. "It was a sort of gesture of defiance."

"Don't you think he drugged Koku with that vapor?"

"No. If he had, Koku would not have been so easily aroused when we approached him. I think the giant just naturally fell asleep and the

Leopard, coming in, saw him that way and so didn't have to use his potion. The scoundrel slipped in, made those spots, and got out again."

"But how did he get over the fence?" asked Ned.

"You're the best one to answer that," Tom remarked with a grim smile. "You say you saw him fly over."

"Well, that's the way it seemed to me."

"He probably did the same thing again tonight. Ned, we must get this man and get him soon. He may strike harder next time."

"That's right, Tom. Oh, if you could only, by some lucky chance, hit on an idea to perfect your television detector and catch this Leopard!"

"I'm pretty close, Ned," Tom said in rather a tired voice. "I think in another few days I can promise some results. I just finished some new cathode ray tubes and they may turn the trick."

"I hope so, Tom."

The two parted, Ned speeding home in his own car. The silence of night settled over the Swift plant and house. Yet in the dark Tom could fancy that a big man, with leopard spots and gleaming eyes, was watching over him.

The next day was a gloomy, rainy one which would have been rather depressing under ordinary circumstances, but the young inventor welcomed it. He had promised Ned to go fishing if the day were fair.

"Now I'll have a good excuse for staying in the laboratory and working on that detector," Tom said. When Ned reported for work, though obviously disappointed in the weather, he, too, decided to put the finishing touches to the secret code, for there were a few loose ends he wished to bind in.

It was late in the afternoon when Ned finished what he was doing, and approaching Tom he asked:

"Are you too busy to make a final test of the code now?"

"Not at all," Tom answered. "I'm rather stuck again, but I think I begin to see daylight. Go down the hall, Ned, and set up your apparatus. I'll take the message on mine here. There's no need of going outside to the lumberyard now."

"No," agreed the manager. "If it works in here it will work outside and for a greater distance. Listen for me now!"

"I hope the Leopard doesn't disturb us again," said Tom with a little smile as Ned left the laboratory.

In a short time the code signals began to come in. Ned was sending generalities, it having been agreed that a message calling for help would not be used in practice. That would be reserved for a time when it was really needed.

"Well, Ned has it down pretty fine," Tom remarked to himself as he sent an answering message. Then, having advised his chum by means of the secret code that it was all but perfect, and calling him to come back to the laboratory, Tom turned again to his work on the television detector.

As Ned entered the laboratory, the manager heard Tom give a loud cry and a moment later saw him leap up and go dancing wildly around the room, excitedly exclaiming:

"I have it! I have it!"

CHAPTER XI

SEEING IN THE DARK

"WHAT'S the matter, Tom? What's the matter?" cried Ned, putting the secret code set on his desk and approaching his chum. "What happened?"

"I have it! I have it!" was all Tom answered, and went on with that strange, wild dance, fairly skipping about the room in what would have been a comical manner had it not seemed so tragic to Ned Newton.

"What do you mean, Tom?" cried the manager. "Have you inhaled some of that poison gas or has the Leopard tried his smoke on you?"

"I have it! I have it!"

"You mean you have my message?"

"I have it! I have it!" repeated Tom, and then Ned fairly shouted:

"What is it? Tell me!"

So imperative were his words that Tom stopped his wild gyrations, leaped toward his chum, clapped him heartily on the back and said:

"Now I have my television detector!"

"Oh," murmured Ned with relief as he sank into a chair. "Well, I don't blame you for doing a war dance. But tell me about it."

"I'll not only tell you, I'll show you!" said Tom. "Just a minute until I jot this down before I forget it."

Tom rapidly made notes of some figures and calculations, and then turned to Ned with a more relieved smile than he had exhibited in some weeks.

"I surely have it now!"

"You mean you have perfected the television detector?"

"Just about. The idea came to me in a flash when you were buzzing out your secret code. You know, of course, that television is due to electrical impulses combined with light waves. That's a crude way of explaining it, but it will do."

"It will for me," Ned said with a laugh. He was no scientist.

"Well," resumed Tom, "I've been bothered with a large blotch of phosphorescent light on my plate where the electrons strike the end of the glass cathode tube. I've been trying to think of some means of getting rid of it, so I can concentrate the television beam and decrease the size of the phosphorescent spot. I've just hit upon the way. You see, when a current of a few amperes flows through the filament it glows and

throws off, perpendicularly to its surface, nega-
tively charged particles so that when——"

"Never mind the details!" interrupted Ned
with a laugh. "The point is, will it work?"

"We'll soon know," said Tom. "I have a few
changes to make in the machine and then I'll let
you see the result of the experiment."

"I'll be waiting for you," Ned answered. "If
we can only trap that Leopard I'll sleep easier
at night."

"We'll get him!" promised Tom Swift.

Tom's conception of "soon" might not agree
with that of most persons, but the next morning
when Ned reported for work he found his chum
busy in the laboratory. On the desk of the young
inventor was a black box with a tube projecting
from one side of it like the tube of a reflex photograph camera. The likeness of the black box to
this type of photographic instrument was further
carried out by a sort of hood or visor on top, a
hood that ended in an oblong piece that took in
the viewer's forehead and eyes. Soft black velvet
excluded all outside light.

"Here's the machine in crude form," Tom
said. "Of course, it's now connected by these
wires to my laboratory current. When I get it
worked out I can put it in a car and use the current from the generator or storage battery. But
this will do for a start."

"Do you mean to say," asked Ned, "that you

can point that jigger at a brick wall, Tom, and
see what goes on beyond it?"

"I mean just that. It's very simple when you
think it out the right way. You know that X-rays
can penetrate almost any substance, as can
radium. Lead offers, at present, the best shield.
But if you stick your hand into an X-ray
machine you can see the bones of your fingers,
which you can't do when you look at your naked
hand.

"The same with a fluoroscope. A doctor stands
you up in front of it and he can look through
you and see your heart beating. This is so ordinary now, though once it wasn't, that no one
wonders at it. I have gone a step further. When
I point this gadget, which looks like a camera,
at a brick wall, or at a wooden or stone one for
that matter, the rays in my machine penetrate
through the barriers, bombard the objects
beyond with electrons, flash back to me and
show themselves on a screen. Here is the screen,"
and Tom indicated a metallic glass one in the
top of the television detector, beneath the hood-
like eye piece.

"I don't see anything yet," Ned said as he bent
over the apparatus.

"I haven't turned on the juice," said Tom,
"but I will in a moment. I want to test it myself
first, and then I'll give you a shot. Go down the
hall to the store room, Ned, and sit at the table.

Do anything you like and I'll see if I can pick it up here on this machine."

"It's something like the photo telephone and your talking picture machine, isn't it?" Ned asked.

"Yes, but in portable form. That's where the hard work comes in—to make a machine we could take around in an auto. And we'll need a car to chase the Leopard."

"You're right, Tom! Well, we'll see how it works."

Ned went to the storeroom, a small apartment at the end of the laboratory building. He closed the door, and sitting down at a table he picked up a box that happened to be standing there and opened it, though there was no special object in his doing this. It contained some old radio tubes that Tom had laid aside.

"If he can look through several walls and see what I'm doing he's pretty good," thought Ned.

To make certain that Tom would have a hard test, Ned turned his back and held the box close to his chest as he opened and shut it several times, took out the tubes, placed them on the table, put them back into the box, and finally hid the chest in a corner under a chair. All this time he was conscious of nothing unusual. If he was being bombarded with unseen X-rays he did not feel them.

There came a knock on the door and Ned,

opening it, saw one of Tom's laboratory assistants standing there.

"Mr. Swift says you are to go back now."

When Ned again entered the laboratory he found Tom dancing about again, but not as wildly as before. There was a look of triumph on the face of the young inventor.

"Did it work?" asked Ned.

"I'll say! And how! Boy, take a look! I'll go there and act for you."

"Could you see all I did?" asked Ned.

"Every motion as plainly as I see you now. Here's what you did," and Tom described every detail of what had taken place, down to the placing of the box under the chair.

"I don't suppose you had somebody spying on me who reported to you, did you?" asked Ned jokingly.

"You can have a shot at it yourself," was Tom's answer, "and then you'll see there's no hocus-pocus about it. Just aim the lens, or what we'll call the lens, in the direction of the room. It's adjusted for distance now. Throw this switch and you'll see what I do through several thicknesses of walls."

Tom hurried to the storeroom. Ned looked through the eye-piece and threw the switch. A strange glow of light suffused the metallic glass screen. There was a low buzzing, humming noise and then, on the plate, just below his eyes, Ned

Newton had a clear vision of Tom Swift two hundred feet away from him and separated from him by several brick and wooden walls. Ned saw Tom walking about the room, rumpling his hair, sitting in a chair, picking up and putting down papers and then going to the corner where Ned had placed the box. Picking the box up Tom looked, as it were, straight at Ned and "made a face" at his chum. It was the climax of success.

"Well," asked Tom as he came back to the laboratory, "could you see me all right?"

"I surely did!"

"And plainly?"

"As sharp as could be. In reduction, of course."

"Oh, yes. I can't get full-sized images on this small apparatus. But this is a big improvement over the first television jigger I made. Then the images were only about an inch square. This is eight by ten and I can make them bigger. But this will do, I think."

"Sure," agreed Ned. "And can you take this machine in a car?"

"Yes. And when I point it at a building I can see all the inmates of it, taking it room by room."

"Then you have to focus it?"

"Sort of, yes. It's like a camera in that respect. To get a view through a building at some distance you need to know, approximately, how far

away the building is. Just as you have to set your camera lens at the proper distance to get a sharp image on the ground glass, you have to set this television detector lens to get the best results. You don't even need to know the distance accurately. You just move the lens in and out until it focuses on the building on which you want to operate. All other objects between will be out of focus, as is the case with a camera, except those with a universal focus. Once you have the object in adjustment on your screen, the forms and actions of all the inmates of a particular room will be visible to you."

"What a machine!" gasped Ned as he visualized the possibilities of what Tom Swift had perfected.

"Yes, I think with this we can catch the Leopard and get back that gas formula. There's only one thing lacking."

"What's that, Tom?"

"To make it operate at night. I had no difficulty in seeing you now for there was sunlight in the room where you were. But we can't expect the Leopard always to be in the light."

"That's right. But what are you going to do about it?"

"I'm on the track of the solution to that part of the problem. It lies in a radium tube. I'm going to attach that to my television detector. The radium rays will shoot out any distance and will

illuminate the persons I want to see without their knowing it. Then I can see them in the dark."

"That's a pretty big order, Tom."

"I can fill it, I think."

It was a week later before Tom was ready to operate his new invention in the dark. Then, one night, he called Ned to the laboratory again and showed him the radium attachment.

"We'll give it a trial," Tom said, "though it has worked once for me. Go to the store room again, Ned, and put out every light."

This Ned did. He was not conscious of what happened, but when he went back to where Tom was working the young inventor described Ned's every act. It was really seeing in the dark.

"Now you try it, Ned," Tom invited.

Ned had his eyes focused on the raised hood of the apparatus and had a glimpse of Tom in the distant dark room. The young inventor was waving his arms, standing on one leg and doing other things that could easily be seen. The television detector had overcome the last difficulty.

"By jinks!" gasped Ned as he realized what a remarkable demonstration he was taking part in. "This is marvelous!" He saw, on the television screen, Tom Swift leaving the dark storeroom. Then, in the blackness of the laboratory Ned felt a hand on his shoulder and a strange voice said:

"I beg your pardon!"

CHAPTER XII

CATCHING MR. DAMON

Startled for the moment, Ned could do nothing but stand there in the darkness beside the television detector, waiting for the next move on the part of the intruding stranger.

"If this is the Leopard, then I'm done for!" thought Ned with wildly-beating heart. Yet he forced himself into a calmer state by recalling that the man's tones had been anything but menacing. They had been gentle and courteous.

His vision temporarily distorted from peering into the visor-like view-finder on the machine, Ned for the moment could make out nothing from the form of his visitor. That he had entered from the corridor was evident, for the door leading to it was open and a faint glow of light came from an incandescent bulb some distance away.

"But how did he get in here past Koku?" mused Ned, for he knew the giant was on guard, or was supposed to be.

Then the unknown visitor or intruder (Ned was not certain into which class to put him) spoke again, saying:

"I beg your pardon. I hope I didn't disturb you. I was told to come in here to find Mr. Swift."

"Who told you?" asked Ned quickly.

"A big man—a regular giant, I should say, at the entrance door."

"Oh, Koku!" murmured the young manager. "Well, he was supposed to keep everybody out. This is a private room and Mr. Swift——"

"I know. I really beg your pardon for coming in, but when your big guard told me to come in here, why, I just came, that's all. I hope I haven't disturbed any of your experiments, Mr. Swift."

"I'm not Tom Swift," said Ned quickly. "He'll be here in a moment. But I don't see how Koku came to let you pass. He has strict orders to let no one in. He got into trouble once and——"

"I'm sorry! I wouldn't for the world make trouble. But I fancy your giant let me in because of seeing this. Look!"

The man, who seemed of ordinary build and not at all like the big, black-bearded foreigner who called himself head of the Leopard League, was now more plainly visible to Ned, whose eyes were assuming their natural focus. The door swung open wider as Tom Swift entered, and in the added light Ned saw gleaming on the man's vest a golden badge on which, in enameled blue letters were the words: "United States Secret Service," followed by a certain number.

"What is it, Ned?" asked Tom Swift quickly, as he entered the room where the television detector stood on a table. "Who is it?" for Tom saw the visitor.

"I don't know," was Ned's reply. "He seems to be from the United States Secret Service——"

"I not only seem to be but I am," was the man's laughing rejoinder, and he did not appear to take offense at Ned's implied doubt. "If you will give us a little more light here I will show you my credentials."

"Oh—all right," said Tom after a moment's pause. "Ned, you know where the main switch is. If you please, give it a push."

Ned stepped past the visitor, and as the clicking of the electric switch threw the laboratory into illumination, Ned saw that in the brief interval Tom Swift had taken the precaution to throw a large dust cloth over the television detector. The young inventor was taking no chances, regardless of his respect for the United States Secret Service.

Then, in the gleam of the electric lights, the three inmates of the laboratory surveyed one another. Tom and Ned, of course, had eyes for no one but their visitor. In his turn he viewed the young men with a disarming smile on his face. A first glance showed Tom and Ned they had nothing to fear. Their visitor inspired confidence. He did more than that, he at once produced proof that he was what he said he was.

"I am Benson Banlot of the United States Secret Service," the man said, introducing himself and again showing his gold badge. "I am connected with the department having charge of deporting undesirable aliens, mostly of the dangerous criminal class. Here are my credentials."

He showed them his identification papers, his warrant of authority from a high United States official, his automobile driver's license and a number of letters addressed to himself.

"Well," said Tom with a smile, "you seem to be what you claim. And if we doubted you, please excuse——"

"Oh, that's all right," interrupted Mr. Banlot. "I don't in the least blame you. You have a right to be assured in every way. I am in need of help and that's why I came to see you, Mr. Swift."

"Help?" exclaimed Tom in some surprise. "Well, it isn't in my line to make any machines for deporting undesirable aliens," and he chuckled a little. "I'm an inventor of mechanical gadgets. Detective work is one of the things I don't know anything about."

"I realize you don't, in the ordinary sense of the word," went on Mr. Banlot. "But I have been sent to this section to locate and arrest a certain foreign criminal who, we have reason to believe, is trying to stir up a form of anarchy against the United States. I have tried without success to find him around here, and on making inquiries I was told that the Swift plant was a large one employing many men, and that there I might find——"

"I hope you don't suspect any of my men!" exclaimed Tom suddenly. "I know them all and I don't believe one of them is an anarchist."

"You never can tell, Mr. Swift," said the Secret Service man. "These fellows work pretty much under cover. I saw, when I came in, a veritable giant on guard at your outer door and——"

"Oh, you can't be after Koku!" cried Tom. "Why——"

"No, no! I was only joking," said Mr. Banlot. "I was going to say if he happened to be the anarchist I was after he would be a most dangerous character. He must be as strong as a bull."

"He is," said Tom, "but he's as gentle as a kitten if you take him right. I don't see how, without a pass, you got beyond him to find your way here."

"I showed him my badge and told him I was a detective police officer, which, in effect, I am," explained Mr. Banlot. "He told me to walk along the hall and I would find you. The place was pretty well deserted but I stumbled in here and I fancy I wasn't altogether welcome," he added with a laugh.

"You did rather startle me," admitted Ned. "You see, Mr. Swift and I were conducting some private experiments and——"

"I hope I didn't spoil anything."

"Oh, no," Tom answered with a glance at the covered television detector. "We had about finished. Of course, I'll be glad to do anything I can to help our country as a whole and you, individually, Mr. Banlot. But I don't see how I can be of service. You are at liberty to go through the plant, to talk to any of the men and——"

"That isn't what I want to do," said Mr. Banlot. "I need your personal help, Mr. Swift. I am told you go about the country a great deal in airships, fast cars and the like. You must come in contact with many persons in different walks of life. It came to my mind that if you would keep your ears and eyes open, as I don't doubt you do, you might get some trace of this man for me. We are sure he is sojourning in this neighborhood. All I want is a tip as to where I can find him and I will make the actual arrest. He is a most dangerous character, working in secret against the safety of the United States."

"Who is this particular man?" asked Tom, and at once it came into his mind, as it did into

Ned's, that Mr. Banlot was after the Leopard. Accordingly, their preconceived ideas received rather a shock when the Secret Service man said:

"This anarchist, to give him one of the bad names he is entitled to, calls himself Alex Kalhofski. I don't suppose that is his real name."

"What sort of looking man is he?" asked Ned.

"He is small and thin, hardly larger than a good-sized boy, and he has a peculiar shade of red hair and beard. Of course, he may dye both, but you can spot dyed hair and beards. Also, he has a livid scar on his left cheek, the result of a premature bomb explosion."

"He can't disguise the scar so easily," remarked Tom.

"No, and by that you may identify him if you ever come across him. But Kalhofski is clever —clever and wicked. He will try to spread his propaganda here and that's what we're afraid of. We want to get him as soon as possible and deport him. May we count on your help, Mr. Swift?"

"Certainly, Mr. Banlot," Tom answered promptly.

"I thought we could," the visitor went on. "That's what I came to find out. My men and I traced Kalhofski to Shopton and here we lost track of him, after what we call a 'hot lead.' If you can help us to pick it up you'll be doing the country a real service."

"I'll do my best," Tom said. "As a matter of fact, I'm looking for a certain man myself. It has nothing to do with anarchy and isn't in your line at all. It's a private matter. But Mr. Newton and I had an idea our man might be in the old automobile factory," and Tom described the brick, barrack-like building where they had seen signs of Twisting Foot. "We haven't been able to find our man there, but you might get on the track of Kalhofski there."

"Thanks! I'll take a look. We generally get in where we want to," said Mr. Banlot with a smile. "It doesn't pay to trifle with Uncle Sam, and if we can help you find your man——"

"Thanks," Tom said, "but it's just a personal matter and I don't want to make it public yet."

"Just as you please," assented the Secret Service man. "But if we can help you any time, let me know."

"I will," Tom said, and when Mr. Banlot had gone the young inventor and Ned talked of his visit before going into a happy confab over the success of the television detector.

"I thought he was going to say he was after our Leopard enemy," remarked Tom.

"So did I," Ned agreed. "He certainly threw a scare into me when he sneaked up on me in the dark and touched me. I thought surely it was the Leopard."

"I'm just as glad it isn't," Tom said. "I want

to get that rascal myself. And I don't want the secret of that deadly gas known, as would happen if the Secret Service men got the formula back for me."

"Kalhofski and this Leopard are two different men," agreed Ned. "We've seen the big, black-bearded chap. He can't shrink into a little man with a red beard."

"No," Tom assented. "Though they're both such criminals, I believe that they may have something in common. Well, how did the detector work, Ned?"

"Perfectly. It sees in the dark all right, Tom."

"Yes, and now we must get busy and try to locate the Leopard with it. I'm tired of having him run around me in circles and probably laughing up his sleeve all the while."

"What's the next move, Tom?"

"To make a new machine like this one, more compact and more efficient," was the answer. "I'll mount it on an auto and we'll start work. This is too big and clumsy for portability. It worked all right in this experimental form, but I need a smaller model for carrying about. It won't take long. It's a success, all right!"

"I'll say it is!" murmured Ned.

Within the next week Tom Swift had completed a new model of his television detector. During that time nothing was seen or heard of the Leopard. There were no more of his uncanny manifestations. In going about Shopton, while the work of making the new model of the detector was in progress, Tom and Ned often met Mr. Banlot. Sometimes he was alone and on other occasions he had one or two men with him. He spoke to the young men, saying there had been no success as yet in locating Kalhofski.

True to his promise, Tom and Ned had done what they could to assist by making guarded inquiries. In some departments of the plant foreigners were employed, and Tom sent an interpreter among them to question them guardedly, but there was no trace of the anarchist, and Tom did not believe his own men would be caught by this bait.

"Well, she's ready!" Tom announced to Ned one day after several hours of hard work. "There she is!" He indicated a new piece of apparatus standing on his desk. It was an oblong box, shaped like a reflex newspaper camera with an adjustable lens tube projecting in front. There was an operating knob on the right side of the box. By turning this the tube could be moved out or in. On top was a hood or visorlike arrangement which shielded the eyes of the observer from outside light. By looking into this visor, which had a bellows like the studio cameras, the observer could see an image thrown upon a metallic glass screen. This was the television image coming from afar, just as Tom

Swift had brought to his photo telephone the picture of the person conversing with him, and also somewhat like his talking picture machine screen. But he had made many improvements.

"This is what makes it see in the dark, Ned," Tom said, pointing to a tube on top of the detector. This tube was something like the periscope of a submarine, only much shorter. It contained prisms and a secret projector in which there was a radium chemical.

"You mean that thing shoots out radium rays," Ned remarked.

"That's it. Radium rays will penetrate anything. They'll bombard the object of our search and illuminate it in the dark. Then we can see the image on this screen."

"It's wonderful, Tom!" exclaimed Ned. "But what are all these gadgets for?" and he indicated various wheels, levers, switches and adjusting devices on the left side of the apparatus.

"That's for enabling us to see into buildings or other places at various distances. Some increase the power of the radium ray, some sharpen the image, some regulate the operating electrical current, for we need electricity to make this work and here's where I plug in to get the current." Tom showed a flexible electrical cord ending in a universal plug.

"Operated in a building or my laboratory," went on Tom, "I can connect this plug with any incandescent light socket. In the automobile I'll connect it with the storage battery or, when the car motor is running, with the generator."

"Can you get current enough that way?"

"Oh, yes. My detector works on the same principle as a wireless short-wave set. Very little current is needed. A twelve-volt storage battery will do the trick. Now we're ready for work, Ned."

"Let's go out and try it!" suggested Ned eagerly. "Let's take a peek at the old barracks, Tom! We may find the Leopard there!"

"Or the red-bearded anarchist!" chuckled Tom. "All right, let's go." Tom picked up the detector which was not very heavy, and was leaving the laboratory with Ned when the telephone rang.

"I'll answer," Ned offered. Tom listened to the one-sided conversation.

"No, Mrs. Damon," Ned spoke, "we haven't seen him in several days. Yes, if he comes in we'll have him call you."

"That was Mrs. Damon," chuckled Ned as he hung up. "She has just come back from her vacation and she wants her funny husband."

"I'm glad he wasn't here," Tom said, laughing. "She might blame us for enticing him away. How's your secret code machine, Ned?"

"All right. It works. I have the pocket set with me now."

"All ready to be kidnapped, eh?" chuckled the young inventor. "Well, I hope you don't have to use it. I wonder what has become of Mr. Damon, by the way?"

"Oh, he's probably off fishing," Ned answered. "If he doesn't get a bite, he'll catch something from his wife when he gets home."

It was dusk when Ned and Tom started out with the television detector temporarily attached to the electric runabout. They were going to the vicinity of the sinister old ruin of a factory building. On the way they passed the town fish store which at this hour was in darkness, but the sight of it reminded Tom that Mrs. Baggert had that afternoon asked him to bring home some lobsters, but he had forgotten about them.

"I'll have hard work to explain this," said Tom ruefully as he halted the car for a moment near the store. "I should have thought of those lobsters."

"Maybe they didn't have any," suggested Ned. "I say, Tom!" he exclaimed, imbued with a sudden idea. "What's the matter with trying the television detector on the fish store?"

"What do you mean?"

"Well, look inside. You can see lobsters as well as anything else. And if you look and don't see any of them, you can truthfully tell your housekeeper there were none."

"But if I do see some?" asked Tom.

"Then we'll have to tell her the truth," spoke Ned. "Go on—take a look!"

"This is a queer way in which to give my detector its first, real test," chuckled the young inventor, "but I'll do it."

The generating wire and plug was quickly inserted into a socket prepared for it on the instrument board of the runabout. Tom made the adjustments and pointed the lens at the fish store which was shrouded in darkness. The radium projector was switched on and Tom peered down into the black velvet bellows hood. He gave a gasp of surprise.

"Did you catch anything?" asked Ned.

"Yes," was the unexpected answer, "I caught Mr. Damon!"

CHAPTER XIII

THE LEOPARD'S LAIR

Ned Newton, for the moment, did not realize what Tom meant.

"What did you say?" asked the manager.

"I said I've caught Mr. Damon!" was the subdued, chuckling reply. "Take a look, Ned!"

Tom made room for Ned at the observing visor, and gazing at the radium-illuminated screen Ned found himself looking through the dark into the interior of the fish shop which was but dimly illuminated by a flickering candle. Even without this light Tom and Ned, by means of the television detector, could have seen what was going on inside, but the candle light was necessary for what Mr. Damon was doing.

"Golly! He's buying some fish!" exclaimed Ned.

"That's what I made him out to be doing," Tom stated. "He's caught all right!"

"What do you mean, Tom?"

"I mean that while his wife was away Mr. Damon slipped off to go fishing. I've heard she doesn't like him to go, though I don't know why. I guess she keeps pretty close tabs on him. Anyhow, when he found he couldn't make any adventure trips with us he decided to go on some by himself. He must have just returned from a fishing trip that wasn't successful. Now he's using a silver hook instead of a steel one, Ned."

"You mean he's buying fish to pretend that he caught them?"

"Yes, to justify himself to his wife. Evidently he has reason to believe she may be at home when he arrives there and he's getting ready to forestall her criticism. How many is he buying?" asked Tom, for Ned had again applied his eyes to the observing hood.

"Half a dozen big ones," reported the manager, for with the television detector he could look through the walls of the fish store and observe everything going on. "He's paying the man now."

Tom's latest invention had no sound device, so only actions could be observed through it. Later he had an idea that he might include sound with the television as is done in the latest radio apparatus now on the market.

"This is great!" chuckled the young inventor. "We've caught Mr. Damon all right. We'll wait until he comes out and hear what he has to say."

They did not have long to wait. Carrying his pole and basket of fish, the eccentric man emerged from a side door of the fish store into the semi-darkness of the Shopton street. His own car was parked a short distance away but before he could go to it Tom called:

"Good evening, Mr. Damon! I see you had very good luck fishing!"

"Bless my fried oysters, Tom Swift, what are you doing here?"

"Just sort of spying on you with the television detector," answered Ned.

"Oh! Oh!" gasped Mr. Damon. "Caught, and fairly! That's a regular infernal machine you have there, Tom Swift! But don't tell my wife! She doesn't want me to go fishing, but if I come home with a good catch she might overlook it. Do you mean to say you saw me there, Tom, buying some fish I couldn't catch?"

"We saw you all right!"

"Bless my spectacles! It doesn't seem possible!"

"Come and take a look, Mr. Damon," Tom invited. So, when the odd little man, smelling very fishy, took his place before the television detector in the runabout, he was allowed to gaze into the interior of the fish shop, the proprietor of which was putting back on ice the finny specimens Mr. Damon had not purchased.

"Marvelous, Tom Swift! Marvelous!" gasped Mr. Damon. "Bless my reel, it doesn't seem possible. And you saw me in there?"

"Every move you made," stated Ned. "But it was just chance. We didn't know you were there," and he and Tom explained how they happened to focus the detector on the fish shop.

"Well, you caught me," said Mr. Damon. "I'm crazy about fishing. I decided to have a go at it while my wife was away but they didn't bite today and I knew she would be home this evening."

"She telephoned us a little while ago," Ned reported.

"Oh! Oh! Well," half moaned the odd man, "I decided the best thing to do would be to buy some fish. So I got Jim Parkman out of his house, had him open his shop and I bought a dozen big, fresh ones. I never thought I'd be caught— spied on in this secret way."

"Beware of Tom Swift's television detector!" warned Ned, laughing.

Mr. Damon was soon on his way home, the two friends promising to keep his secret. They wished him well. Then, the detector having been turned off, Tom and Ned drove on to the barracks, as they called the old building.

"I wonder if we'll see anything?" murmured Ned as they went their way toward the slum section of Shopton.

"We'll see something, sure!" Tom declared. "We've already proved that we can look through the side of a building in the dark and see what is going on. Whether we'll find the Leopard or that anarchist is another question."

"I don't believe the red-bearded anarchist will be there," Ned gave as his opinion. "If he had been, Banlot and his Secret Service men would have nabbed him by this time."

"Perhaps," Tom admitted. "Anyhow, we'll soon know."

They drove forward cautiously, for by this time the electric runabout was no doubt pretty well known to the inhabitants of the old shack. Tom Swift did not want to take any chances.

"Well, here we are!" remarked the young inventor in a low voice as they drove into a secluded, dark lane several hundred feet away from the old building.

"The lair of the Leopard," murmured Ned as Tom stopped the car.

"We'll soon know whether or not he's there," said the young inventor as he began to adjust the television detector.

CHAPTER XIV

THE CRYSTAL CAVE

SILENCE and darkness seemed to surround the old ruin of a building as Tom Swift and his chum prepared what might well be a supreme test of the television detector. There was no sign of life about the "lair of the Leopard," as Ned had dubbed the place. It might be, and probably was teeming with life, but there was no outward indication of it. The inmates preferred the darkness.

"Doesn't seem to be much activity around there," Tom said in a low voice as he plugged the electric cord into the socket prepared for it.

"Not yet," Ned agreed. "But if we happen to see the Leopard with your formula, Tom, what are you going to do about it?"

"Go in and get it, of course. That's too dangerous a secret to let remain in such unscrupulous hands."

"Go in and get it!" gasped Ned. "You mean now—we two? Of course I'll back you up, Tom, but——"

"I guess we'd need help, Ned," Tom agreed.

"I'm not going to rush into danger. Once we locate that scoundrel, I'll go get Koku and some of our men and raid the place. I don't want the police or Secret Service men in on this. They'd ask too many questions and the quieter I can keep the knowledge of that gas formula the better I'll like it."

"Then the thing to do," suggested the manager, "is to make sure the Leopard is in there?"

"That's right."

"And maybe the red-bearded anarchist."

"Oh, I don't believe he's there, or otherwise Banlot would have located him by this time. I guess Kalhofski got a tip that he was wanted and skipped out."

"Maybe. Well, are you almost ready?"

"Almost. I want the tubes to warm up before I focus on the building. The radium device isn't working as strongly as I'd like it to, but I think it will give us light enough. I must make some adjustment to that part of my detector tomorrow or the next day."

The two sat in the car, waiting in silence. The only sounds they heard were the sighing of the night wind and the noises made by the insects that come with darkness. It was a warm, calm night, very dark, for clouds hid the moon and there seemed to be a storm brewing.

"I guess it's ready now," Tom said in a low voice. "Stand by, Ned! On your guard!"

"Why?" asked the manager. "You don't think they'd rush us, do you?"

"There's no telling. Of course, my detector works silently and those whom we hope to observe in that old shack will not know we are looking at them. But after what happened the other night I want to be prepared."

"You mean the night the Leopard spotted the runabout?"

"That's it—yes. There's something sinister about this darkness. I have a strange feeling that we are going to be observed as well as observing. So stand by while I take a look and focus the machine."

Tom bent over the observing hood of his machine. The double-anode, high-vacuum, cathode-ray oscillograph tubes were well warmed now by the electric current flowing into them from the car storage battery.

Tom Swift pointed the radium projector tube at the stone wall outside the dark and silent building. Its invisible rays flowed through the wall and through the brick, wood and plaster, penetrating every room.

Before Tom could look into the observing hood a strange thing happened. So powerful was the new machine that the mysterious rays shooting through the stone wall reflected back and showed upon the outside a picture of the scene behind.

"Look, Tom!" exclaimed Ned. "Did you think it would do that?"

"No, I didn't," said Tom.

What they saw was a bearded man leaning over in a sinister posture.

"If we can see that without looking down on the reflecting screen," said Tom, "it shows that this machine ought to be pretty good. Now I am going to try it."

With his eyes peering into the observing hood, the young inventor now began to turn the knob on the right side of the box-like instrument to adjust the lens tube, or what would have corresponded to a lens tube on a camera. Tom aimed his detector at the top story of the building, intending to search each floor thoroughly for a view of the Leopard.

Slowly he moved the tube from left to right, taking in all of the top floor of the old building. A murmur of chagrin told Ned, without words, that the result was negative. On the alert, the manager looked behind and around the car into the darkness. There was no sign of any foe.

Tom lowered the tube to the floor beneath the top one. This time he uttered an exclamation of satisfaction.

"Is he there?" asked Ned in cautious tones.

"No, he isn't, but there's a gang of tramps there playing some kind of a card game. Take a look."

Ned did as directed and bent over the television detector. No sooner had he looked into the black velvet visor, than he saw on the screen a clear view of what was going on inside the building.

Through the brick, wood and plaster walls Ned could see as easily as a doctor does through the fluoroscope the beating of his patient's heart; more plainly, in fact, for the fluoroscope at best gives but a shadowy image. In the television detector Ned could note every form and shape, even to the color of the garments, the hair and beards of the frowsy tramps, though their images were reduced in size.

These irresponsible members of society were holding what for them were high revels on one of the floors of the old factory. Half a score sat about on boxes or barrels, and around a table illuminated by a kerosene lantern hanging above it were five men playing cards. They seemed to be having a good time, if actions meant anything, and on the unshaven faces were grins of mirth. Of course, no sound came to either Tom or Ned.

"Golly, it's as plain as day," murmured Ned.

"It surely is!" Tom agreed. "I guess I've made a better machine than I figured on, Ned!"

"Indeed you have. There was a bearded man but I doubt if he was the Leopard."

"Well, we have more floors to spy upon."

It was, in truth, spying, but entirely justifiable in its purport. The boys were working toward a good end and doing no harm to the unfortunate castaways who were congregated in the old barracks.

Tom took another view of the interior scene which his detector and the radium rays made as visible to him and his chum as though the structure had walls of glass. He chuckled at some of the antics of the homeless men and then moved the tube down so he could see into another floor.

Here, too, were more tramps, and some that did not look as harmless as the ordinary "hoboes," for in one corner of a room evil-appearing men sat with their heads together as if plotting some daring crime.

Thus, floor after floor of the Leopard's lair was explored by means of Tom Swift's marvelous machine but there was no trace of either man wanted—the one that might be made to give up the secret formula he had stolen, the other that might be sent away from the country that generously harbored him and against which he was secretly plotting.

"Well, I guess we drew blanks this time," Tom remarked as he cut off the power and got ready to move the car.

"Nothing doing tonight," agreed Ned. "But the next time we come he may be here."

The detector which as yet was not permanently fitted to the car was taken down and stowed away, and as Tom took his seat at the wheel to go back to the laboratory Ned, turning suddenly toward a clump of bushes in the rear, exclaimed:

"Who's there? Come out!"

There was no reply—no movement.

"What was it?" asked Tom in a low voice.

"I thought I heard someone in there," Ned answered. "Maybe it was a stray cat, though."

"Wait a second!" whispered Tom. The runabout was equipped with a small, but powerful searchlight. The young inventor quickly switched this on and focused the dazzling beam upon the bush Ned was regarding with suspicion. Not even a mouse could have come out from it without having been detected and no person could have remained in hiding back of it.

"I guess there's nothing there," Ned remarked with a sigh of relief after several tense seconds of waiting.

"Lucky for someone it isn't!" said Tom grimly. "Well, let's go!"

They were soon back at the laboratory and the television detector was carried inside. Then, as Ned was about to go on home in the electric runabout which stood in the shop yard beneath a brilliant light, he and Tom made a discovery that startled and alarmed them.

"Look!" murmured Ned, pointing to a yellow smear on one of the side doors. "The Leopard's spot again."

"That's it!" gasped Tom as he recognized the peculiar thumb mark. "He must have been there in the dark after all."

"And he left us his trade-mark," added Ned. "He must have sneaked up on us while we were looking into the detector. I was sure I heard some movement in that bush."

"Well, he got away!" said Tom with a trace of chagrin in his voice. "He's fooled us again. We must get that man!"

"And we will!" declared Ned. "But say, Tom, maybe that's an old mark—from the last time the Leopard spotted us, I mean."

"No, I had all traces cleaned off. Besides, this is fresh. Look!"

With his fingers Tom rubbed away part of the Leopard's yellow thumb mark. His fingers were stained with some sort of damp coloring matter. The spot had only recently been put on the car and it could not be doubted but that it had been affixed while the auto had been parked in the lonely spot during the television operations.

"I'll have this stuff analyzed," Tom declared, removing the remainder of the mark onto a clean handkerchief. "It may give us a clue and we surely need it! This Leopard is a fast and dangerous worker, jumping over my fence and so on. We must get him, Ned!"

"And we shall!"

"Maybe you'd better take one of the men with you, Ned," Tom suggested as his chum was about to drive to his home.

"Why?"

"Well, it might be dangerous. They may try to hold you up."

"I'm not afraid."

"No, but I'm afraid for you, Ned. I'll send Koku and one of the men home in the runabout with you and they can bring the car back. We won't take any chances."

Though Ned rather laughed at this precaution, he did feel a bit easier with the big giant riding beside him and one of Tom's night guards in the rumble-seat. The trip back and forth was made without incident, however.

Next morning when Ned reported at the laboratory, he found Tom busy with a microscope and test tubes, glass slides and other apparatus at his big desk.

"What's up now?" Ned inquired. "Improvements to the television detector?"

"No, though I have found a way to make the radium rays stronger. This time I'm trying to figure out what sort of stuff it was the Leopard used to mark the car, Ned."

"Have you found out?"

"Yes, it's a peculiar kind of sticky, yellow clay in a natural state, I believe. Something like yellow ocher."

"Yellow ocher!" exclaimed Ned. "You mean the yellow clay that's used in mixing paints?"

"It seems to be that, Ned. Take a look. You've done some microscopic work, haven't you?"

"A little, yes."

"Here is some genuine yellow ocher I got from our paint shop for comparison."

Ned put his eye to the fine machine Tom had adjusted for him. Magnified greatly was a smear of yellow on a glass slide below the object glass. Ned made a mental picture of the stuff left by the Leopard and then took a look at what was known to be yellow ocher.

"Well?" asked Tom as his chum looked up.

"They're both ocher," Ned declared, "but not from the same source of supply. The grains are neither the same shape nor size."

"I noticed that."

"Unless I'm greatly mistaken, Tom, I know where the ocher came from with which the Leopard spotted our car."

"You do! Where?"

"From the crystal cave!"

"You mean that cave about five miles out of town?"

"Yes, just back of Walnut Creek. There's

yellow ocher there in a natural state. I remember when I was a kid going after crystals and getting the stuff all over my pants. That yellow ocher is from the crystal cave, all right! I'm sure of it!"

"Then," said Tom in a low voice, "this may mean the Leopard is hiding there."

"He may be, Tom!"

"Then I'm going to turn my television detector on the crystal cave! Come on!"

CHAPTER XV

THE ESCAPE

ELATED by what seemed to be the most promising clue yet leading in the direction of the Leopard, Tom and Ned stood in the laboratory and enthusiastically shook hands.

"We have him!" cried the manager.

"Not quite yet, but I think we're on his trail, thanks to what you just told me about that ocher being in the crystal cave," said the inventor.

"Oh, that was only added information," Ned went on. "It was your cleverness in deciding to analyze the stuff from which the yellow smears were made that turned the trick."

"Enough of compliments!" chuckled Tom. "Let's get to work."

"You mean to go to the crystal cave now and find out, with your television detector, whether or not the Leopard is hiding there, Tom?"

"Not now exactly, Ned, but as soon as it's dark. I want to work as quietly as I can. But let's get ready."

"Sure!" agreed the manager.

First the television machine was carefully gone over. Tom had planned some improvements, especially in the radium projector, and he and Ned wanted to test out the delicate but powerful machine which could "see" through a brick wall.

"If the Leopard is in the cave, what are you going to do?" asked Ned as he and his chum worked together in the laboratory. "I mean if you see him there."

"We're going in and get him!" declared Tom stoutly. "At least I'm going to take away that gas formula from him."

"Yourself?" Ned's voice showed his concern.

"Well, I'll have you help and Koku and some of the men."

"Then you won't call in the police or the Secret Service men?"

"Not yet. I may have to if we fail, but I don't believe we shall. I'm depending on you, Ned."

"Oh, I'll help in any way I can, but when it comes to tussling with a six and a half foot foreigner, who has a beard like a hair mattress and who can leap over a fifteen-foot fence, I beg to be excused."

"I'll let Koku do the heavy work," chuckled Tom. "At the same time I'd like to know how that fellow got over my fence when he found he couldn't get under it."

"Ask him and maybe he'll tell you."

"I shall. What I meant when I said I depended on you, was about the location and layout of the cave itself. You say you've been there?"

"Not lately, but I used to go there often with the other boys when I was a kid," Ned admitted. "Didn't you?"

"I don't believe I was ever in the crystal cave," Tom answered. "I never seemed to have the time. I know where it is, though. But it's the inside I want to know about to better use the detector outside."

Ned sketched as well as he could remember the formation of the cavern which had a local reputation as a place of mystery. It was not very large but extended back into a hill on the east bank of Walnut Creek. The interior of the cave was made of some kind of rock, Ned reported, and in places there were stalactites which glittered when a light was thrown on them, thus giving the cave its crystal name.

"We boys used to break off these crystals," Ned went on, "so I don't imagine there are many left."

"The Leopard and those with him probably don't care for such things," spoke Tom as he tested the improved radium ray projector and found it much more powerful.

"How do you size up the situation?"

"I think the Leopard, and possibly some

friends of his, began to find the barracks too hot for them," Tom answered. "You know, the Secret Service men have been there several times looking for 'Red-Beard', which we'll call him for short—you know this Kalhofski."

"Oh, I get you!" exclaimed Ned. "You mean the undesirables skipped out and went to live in the cave?"

"Yes," Tom agreed. "That's what I think. And finding some yellow clay there which suited his purpose in making his threatening marks, the Leopard took some. It's lucky for us he did, but it may be unlucky for him. I wish I had analyzed the stuff with which the first spots were made. But probably it was some other kind of material."

The detector was now working well. It was more powerful than ever as Tom and Ned proved in daylight. Ned went to a distant part of town where, even though he was behind the brick wall of a building Tom was able to pick him out by television and describe his every action.

"It's great, Tom!" Ned exclaimed on his return. "To what distance will your machine work?"

"There's practically no limit to it any more than there is to a short-wave wireless, or there won't be when I get it perfected," was the answer. "Just now it will work up to a few miles with good results, and with excellent results within a mile or less."

"You sort of have to focus it for distance, don't you, Tom?"

"In a measure, yes. That's why I sent you to the Barnstable Building just now. I knew, to within a few feet, just how far that was from here and I could focus accordingly. That's why I want to go to crystal cave in daylight and pick out a place where we can take our position tonight. Then I'll have the distance fairly exact. The detector will work better that way."

Last minute adjustments were made, there was a final test of the machine in the laboratory, and then Tom and Ned late in the afternoon drove to crystal cave, leaving the television detector in the laboratory under guard of Koku, who had strict orders to let no one approach it, not even the men in the plant.

"I hope nothing happens to it while we're gone," Ned remarked as he and Tom were on their way to the cave.

"They'll have to kill Koku to damage it," was the answer.

"The Leopard might knock him out again with that queer dope."

"I don't believe that will happen," Tom responded.

There was no sign of life about the crystal cave when the two young men walked toward it after parking the car some distance away. The entrance was a short distance up the hill from the stream, the approach being made by a rough, overgrown path. Weeds and bushes almost hid the opening.

"The cave isn't visited much any more," Ned remarked as he and Tom decided on a vantage place screened from observation where they could halt the car with the television detector that night.

"But there have been men coming and going here," Tom declared, pointing to footprints in the soft soil of the path.

"Yes," Ned agreed. "And the Leopard may be up there now."

The two gazed toward the cavern entrance, but there was no sign of life visible. All was sinister silence. Night was the time of activity for the Leopard and his whelps. By day they slept.

"Well, we might as well get back," Tom decided when he and his chum had measured the distance as well as they could calculate it from the cave entrance to where they would park the car after dark. "I must arrange my raiding party."

"It will be a sort of raid, won't it?" chuckled Ned.

The detecting machine was attached for the night excursion to a powerful touring car instead of to the runabout. This would give room to take Koku and several husky men from the shop. Tom selected his helpers with care. Night came, and under a nervous tension the party got into the car, with Ned and Tom on the front seat, the former at the wheel, the latter at the controls of the television apparatus.

They drove along in the darkness and Tom was glad that there was no moon, for he did not want to be discovered near the cave before he had a chance of spying into it.

"Hold the car here a moment, Ned," Tom said in a low voice as they neared the old barrack building.

"You don't think the Leopard is in here, do you?"

"No, but I want to test the improved machine in the dark, and it's just as well, anyhow, to make sure the man we want isn't here. It won't take but a minute or two."

The car was halted in a secluded spot. Tom, turning on the current, focused the seeing "eye" of his machine on the brick ruin. Room after room he looked into as before, but the man he sought was not there.

"Just a few tramps lolling around," Tom reported as he shut off the power. "Now we'll go on to the cave."

The neighborhood of the cavern was a deserted and lonely spot and there was no activity about it when the auto cautiously approached. It took but little time to park in the selected place, and then, telling Koku and the others to be on the alert, Tom Swift once more started his apparatus working and focused it on the secret crystal cave. It took several seconds for the anode tubes to warm up, but when they were glowing with the subdued light that operated them, Tom gazed into the eye visor. He uttered an exclamation.

"Is he there?" exclaimed Ned.

"See here!" was the answer.

Ned bent down, looked upon the reflecting screen, and as Tom had done gave a low murmur of satisfaction. He could look into the cave almost as clearly as though he stood within its entrance. The place was not altogether in darkness for here and there candles gleamed and there were several lanterns hung up in different parts, making the stalactites glitter.

Seen thus were several men. Some were eating at box tables, some were stretched out on piles of old bags, seemingly asleep, but it was the sight of one man sitting at a rude table, illuminated by a lantern hung above it, that had caused Tom and Ned to exclaim. For there was the black-bearded foreigner of extraordinary bulk and height. There could be no mistaking him even had he not worn on a chain about his neck a badge engraved with the image of a crouching animal. On the table in front of him was a small box.

"The Leopard!" murmured Ned as he looked up.

"The Leopard!" confirmed Tom Swift. "And he has my secret formula. The box isn't open yet and if we act quickly enough it may not be. Koku, Larsen, Dubfold, get ready!" he warned the men. "You're going to help us raid that place!"

"We ready, Master!" rumbled the giant, eagerly.

Tom took another look through the television machine. The Leopard was alone in the middle of the crystal cave tinkering with the little chest which evidently baffled his efforts to open it. Doubtless the Latin warning kept him from smashing it. The other inmates of the cavern seemed to be paying no attention to the black-bearded foreigner. There was no sign of Red-Beard, as Tom and Ned noted.

Leaving one man on guard at the machine, Tom, Ned and the others of the raiding party, with Koku carrying a big club which he said he would rather use than a gun, cautiously approached the cave. Their plans had been well laid but the best of plans often fail, as Tom and his force soon discovered.

Whether there were concealed wires which conveyed a signal to those in the cave, or whether some lookout hiding in the dark bushes gave notice of the approach, they could not make sure. But as they gathered at the weed-grown entrance and started inside there came a warning shout from someone within, all lights went out suddenly, there was a rush of feet away from, not toward, the raiders, and when a few seconds later Tom Swift's party entered the cave, it was empty.

"He's escaped!" cried Ned as he flickered his powerful flashlight about the glittering cavern.

"Yes," echoed Tom, bitterly, "he got away."

"They all escaped, it seems," said one of the men.

"There must be a back exit to this place," remarked another.

"There must be," Ned admitted, "though I never heard of it."

"Me kotch um!" rumbled Koku, starting toward the dark rear of the cave.

"No!" cried Tom Swift, flashing his light on the table where the Leopard had been sitting, "I've found what I came for!"

He held up the secret box.

CHAPTER XVI

A SINISTER WARNING

STRANGE was the scene as Tom Swift stood in the crystal cave, holding aloft the stolen secret box which he had been able to discover by the aid of his television detector. About him were grouped Ned Newton and the husky men led by Koku who had hoped to come to grips with the Leopard. But the foreigner had fled.

"Is the box all right, Tom?" asked Ned anxiously. "I mean, has it been opened?"

"Doesn't seem so," was the answer. "No, I don't believe it has. I'll make sure as soon as we get back to the laboratory. I don't want to work the secret catch here," he added in a low tone.

"Aren't we going to chase after these fellows, Mr. Swift?" asked one of the men who seemed eager for a fight.

"No," was the answer. "We don't know what may lie back of this cave, and now that I have what I came for we'll leave."

"Me like punch somebody," rumbled Koku. "Man what make smoke in my eyes."

"I've no doubt you'd like to come to grips with him," observed Tom, "and I want to see him punished for what he has done. I wish I could find out certain things he knows. But he's escaped and I don't believe we'll be troubled with him any more. Let's go!"

They left the cave to its darkness and to the possible menacing inhabitants thereof who might have only retreated to the labyrinth in the back, possibly the Leopard among them. But Tom Swift did not want to take the risk of any of his men being injured.

The raiding party, successful in the better half of its objective, was soon back at the Swift plant. There, in the seclusion of the laboratory, Tom and Ned examined the box which Ned saw for the first time.

"It's all right!" cried Tom exultantly as he pressed the secret catch which opened the container. "It hasn't been damaged and here is the secret formula. So I guess it hasn't been opened."

"How do you know?" asked Ned.

Tom pointed to an intricate seal he had placed on the paper wrapper which contained the details of the instructions for making the deadly gas. It had not been disturbed.

"The Leopard could not open the box after he stole it from my vault," Tom went on. "He tried, though," and he showed Ned certain marks and scratches which indicated that some instrument had been used on the strange casket. "Probably if he had it a little longer he would have become impatient, and ignoring the Latin warning would have smashed the box to get at the papers inside. Then the fat would have been in the fire for keeps."

"Do you think he knew what was in the box?" Ned inquired.

"I'm pretty sure he did. No one would have taken the trouble to enter my secret vault just to get this box, unless he knew what it contained."

"Then he must have had some knowledge of what he was after."

"Too much knowledge," Tom answered rather gloomily. "I don't see how he managed to get in my vault which I thought no one could open. I can't imagine how he even knew it existed. And furthermore, I can't figure out how he knew of Alhazar's secret formula. When I bought it from him he said that he alone knew about it."

"It's strange," Ned agreed. "And now that the Leopard has escaped we'll probably never know those answers."

"I'm not going to let it rest there," Tom Swift went on. "I'm still going to use my television detector to try to locate that rascal. I'm not done with him yet!"

"Good!" exclaimed Ned. "I'll help you."

The secret formula was again placed in the vault, and with the new locks and the extra precautions he had taken Tom felt sure the method of making the deadly gas would never become known. His theory was that some man, perhaps the head of the Leopard League, wanted the secret in order to make wholesale killings and thus overturn some government in Europe.

"There is always scrapping over there, in some place or other," Tom remarked to Ned. "If some radicals used the gas over there, it would be only a step before they might try to use it here. It must never be done!"

"Never!" agreed the manager.

How the story got out neither Tom nor Ned knew, for they had cautioned Koku and the members of the raiding party against talking. But some of the papers got hold of the tale and made it fantastic by relating how Tom Swift, "the eminent young inventor," had by using a new and marvelous machine recovered a considerable sum of money which had been stolen from him and secreted in the crystal cave.

"I'm glad they think it's money and know nothing about the gas formula," Tom remarked to Ned as they read the stories. "Let it go that way."

"But Tom, the secret of your television detector is out now!"

"Well, I didn't intend to keep that a secret. I think it's good enough to patent and sell. I'm not concerned about that. As long as they don't spring the secret gas formula, I'm satisfied."

"How do you suppose the story got out?"

"Oh, I guess some of the men talked in spite of my warning. I don't know that I can blame them. It was quite an adventure, and naturally they spoke of it afterward. Then, too, we might have been observed going into the cave. We couldn't keep that a secret. No, I'm satisfied to let the public know about the detector."

In the next few days the papers contained many stories, some far-fetched and very fantastic, about the new television detector. Tom granted interviews to reporters and told them and showed them just what the apparatus would do. But of course he said nothing about the gas formula, letting the impression remain that he had given his machine the first practical test in recovering a large sum of money.

"We know that isn't just what happened," Tom said to Ned, "and the Leopard knows it. But as long as he doesn't talk, and I don't believe he will, now that we've beaten him, the gas formula is safe. Let it go that way."

"Sure!" agreed Ned.

Then came another visit from Benson Banlot.

"That's a wonderful machine you have, Mr. Swift," began the Secret Service man.

"Well, yes, it worked pretty well," Tom admitted, smiling.

"I wonder if you wouldn't let it help us, and incidentally your own country," went on the operator.

"Why, of course," Tom said quickly. "What is it?"

"Well, we haven't yet been able to catch that anarchist. He slips through our nets every time. Now, if you can see through a brick wall and locate a bandit who took your money, Mr. Swift, maybe you can locate this little red-bearded runt for us. I'm sure he's still in this neighborhood. Will you help us?"

"Yes, I will, Mr. Banlot," was the answer. "I'll be glad to and I'll start in at once."

"Good! Then here's the information," and the Secret Service man told Tom and Ned all that was known of the criminal who was being sought for deportation. There was a long conference and certain plans were made. Tom agreed to make several trips about the country surrounding Shopton, concentrating on localities where Kalhofski was known to have been, to try to locate him in some secret haunt. Mr. Banlot or some of his men would go with Tom and Ned at times, and on other occasions the two young men would go alone.

"And I wish you luck!" said Mr. Banlot as he parted from Tom.

"We may need it," answered the young inventor.

But luck seemed in hiding during the next week. In company with Secret Service operators, though more often by themselves, Tom and Ned went about the country making many night trips and focusing the television detector on suspected places. Many dangerous men were thus spied upon, but there was no trace of "Red-Beard," nor did the Leopard again show his spots.

"I'm afraid he's given us the slip," Tom remarked to Ned one night after a fruitless day's search.

"It does seem so," his chum agreed, bending over his pocket wireless set on which he was practicing the secret code. "But it isn't our business, anyhow."

"It's our business to help our country in any way we can!" said Tom.

"Oh, yes, of course," Ned agreed. "But I mean it isn't as if this anarchist had your gas formula."

"He may be almost as dangerous as the Leopard was when he had it," went on the young inventor. "Thanks to the television detector, we cut the Leopard's claws. But the anarchist is still a menace and we're going to get him."

"I hope so, Tom. I'll do all I can to help."

The all-seeing machine was temporarily locked in the secret vault and Tom and Ned prepared to leave the laboratory, having made plans for another search in a day or two.

As they opened the door to go into the hall, a paper, which seemed to have been fastened to the knob, fell to the floor.

"What's this?" asked Ned as he picked it up.

Tom took it, read it at a glance, and exclaimed:

"It's a warning and a bad one! Look!"

Ned quickly scanned the few words:

"Keep away from us, Tom Swift, if you want your friend Ned Newton to go on living. This is our last warning. League of the Leopard."

CHAPTER XVII

KIDNAPPED

For a moment there was tense silence between the two friends. Then Ned exclaimed:

"I think it's all bunk!"

"Bunk!" murmured Tom Swift.

"Yes, this is a joke. There must be some of your men, Tom, who like this particular form of fun. Probably they left this here as a joke."

"Do you call that a joke?"

Tom indicated several smeary yellow thumb prints on the bottom of the paper.

"The spots of the Leopard," he murmured.

"Oh, I didn't see those," Ned admitted. "Well, it does seem as if that beast had been around again."

"But how could he get in here?" demanded Tom. "Koku!" he called, summoning the giant who had been on guard when the two friends entered the laboratory.

"Here, Master!" came the answer.

Tom and Ned saw the big native entering the laboratory front door which opened upon a private yard.

"Where have you been?" demanded Tom rather sternly. "You were supposed to be on guard here, Koku."

"Sure, Master. Koku on guard. But hear um noise and go out see what it was. Only cats fighting."

Tom glanced quickly at Ned and remarked:

"I can guess what happened. The Leopard was here. He must have got over the fence in his own mysterious way. Then he imitated a noise which he figured would draw Koku away from his post, while he slipped in and left the warning. He's beaten us again, Ned!"

"It seems so! Did you see anything wrong, Koku, or anybody?" he asked.

"No see anybody—only cats fighting—not see um—hear um," was the answer.

"That's how it happened," Ned agreed. "Tom, we've a dangerous man to deal with."

"I knew that some time ago," was the calm answer. "But what do you make of this warning against yourself, Ned?"

"Bluff! I'm not afraid. They're trying to scare you. But don't worry. They won't kill me."

"No, but they may——"

"They won't even get me!" boasted Ned. "And if they do——"

"Well, if they do?"

"I've my pocket wireless set to summon help,

Tom. I'll let you know by the secret code where I am if they get me and you can come and save me."

"I hope I can, Ned. Don't ever be without that sending set. I'll be on the alert if anything should happen to you."

"Oh, don't worry! Nothing will happen. But are you going to let this scare you off?" and Ned indicated the warning.

"Would you?"

"Certainly not!"

"Then I won't either, Ned. I'm going after that anarchist and the Leopard harder than ever!"

"I'm with you, Tom! We'll defy these beasts!"

It was thought best to acquaint the Secret Service men with what had happened. This was done the next day, when Mr. Banlot called. Though Tom said nothing about the gas formula, he told Mr. Banlot what had happened and showed him the warning against Ned Newton.

"Leopard League, eh?" murmured the Secret Service man. "That's a new one on me. I don't believe it has anything to do with that anarchist we're after, but the two may be banded together. As for this warning, don't let it frighten you."

"We're not going to."

"Only take precautions," advised Mr. Banlot.

"We'll do that," Ned answered. "I'm not afraid. They can't strike at Tom through me!"

"They're desperate beasts," went on Mr. Banlot. "But we'll beat 'em at their own game. How's the television detector working?"

"Fine," Tom replied, "though it hasn't yet picked up Red-Beard!"

"You'll get him. Keep at it!"

This Tom and Ned did but with no results. The detector rendered good assistance, however, in locating a number of criminals wanted by the Secret Service men, by revealing the desperate men in their haunts.

They were arrested, some being sent to jail and others deported. But the master-mind, the dangerous, red-bearded anarchist slipped through the net every time. Once Tom and Ned were sure they had a glimpse of him in a gang of shaggy, unshaven outcasts hiding in a veritable den, but of this they could not be certain because of the jumbled throng of human beings. When the Secret Service men finally arrived, they found the place deserted.

So the search went on, baffling and uncertain, until Ned was almost ready to call it off. But Tom Swift persisted. In all this time they neither saw nor heard anything from the Leopard.

One morning Ned did not appear at the

laboratory, though he had promised to come early, for there were some new experiments to try out. Tom waited, then telephoned his manager's house.

"He left some time ago," was the report.

"That's strange," Tom mused. "If he started he should be here unless something happened. In that case he would have telephoned. If he were in an accident I should have heard about it."

Uneasy in his mind, Tom got out his own car and went to Ned's home on the other side of town. There was no trace of him, but knowing the route his manager generally took in coming to the office Tom went over the same ground. There was a short cut through a meadow and patch of woods that Ned often used when in a hurry, and guessing that he might have gone that way Tom turned his car into what was rather a lonely stretch of seldom-used road.

Tom's worst fears were confirmed, when in the middle of the woodland patch he came upon Ned's car off to one side of the road, showing evidence of having been forced there to make a sudden stop. There were skid marks of the tires in the soft dirt.

"But there was no smash!" Tom murmured as he got out to make a closer inspection. "So I guess Ned wasn't hurt. Maybe he summoned the police and had some careless motorist arrested. He may have gone to police head-quarters. I'll call up."

Before doing this, however, Tom looked carefully into Ned's car. Then he saw evidences of a struggle. One of the front seats was partly pulled out, there was a rent in the upholstery, and a small tool compartment on one side of the instrument board was open as if Ned had tried to get a wrench or a pair of pliers with which to defend himself.

But more sinister than anything else were three marks of a smeary thumb on the inside of the windshield.

"The Leopard's spots!" exclaimed Tom. "The worst has happened! Ned has been kidnapped!"

Nobody had actually seen Ned kidnapped. He had passed along the lonely way early in the morning, had been picked up by the sinister men, and that was the last heard of him. There was worry and consternation, of course. Tom's wife was in tears as she sought to comfort Helen Morton, a young lady whom Ned hoped to marry some day.

"Don't worry, Helen," urged Mrs. Swift. "Tom will find Ned."

"Oh, I hope so," sighed Helen.

Mr. Banlot came to the laboratory to consult with Tom the night of the day on which the kidnapping took place.

"Any news?" asked the Secret Service man hopefully.

"None," answered Tom despondently. "I guess we had better go out with the television detector. It may help."

"I'm sure it will!" the government sleuth declared. "I'll get a couple of men and——"

"Hark!" suddenly cautioned Tom. "Someone is coming."

There were footsteps in the corridor outside the laboratory.

CHAPTER XIX

IN CAPTIVITY

WHEN Ned Newton arose early that fateful morning, his mind was filled with the many plans he expected to help Tom Swift carry out that day. There was much to be done in the laboratory besides aiding the government men in locating the anarchist.

"If they ask my opinion," murmured Ned as he finished his breakfast and went to get his car, "I'd say, they'll never catch Red-Beard around here. I think he's skipped with the Leopard, and I'm glad of it."

There came to Ned's mind the memory of the warning note, but he only laughed.

"They don't dare do anything," he told himself.

Driving along through Shopton, Ned happened to glance at a clock which made him realize that he was a bit late.

"My watch must be slow," he said. "I'll take the short-cut. Tom may be waiting for me."

So fate, if that is what Ned's slow watch may be called, took a hand in the proceedings, though

it was later learned it would have made no difference had Ned gone the longer and more
regular route. The same thing would have happened, for he was being trailed.

It was not until the manager was on the
short-cut and speeding his car toward the little
patch of woods that Ned noticed another
machine approaching him from the rear. This
was a matter of some surprise to him, for the
road he was on was seldom traveled.

"Must be somebody else in a hurry," mused
Tom's chum.

The other auto soon overtook Ned. Then, to
the surprise and alarm of the manager, the
machine swung so close to him that it forced
him to swerve to the right.

"Hey! What do you think you're doing?" Ned
angrily demanded as he jammed on the brakes,
for there was a deep ditch just ahead and he
did not want to go into that with the danger of
overturning.

"We don't think—we know what we're doing!" snapped an ugly-faced man, leaning out
of the right side of the touring car which was
coming to a stop. "We want you!"

In a flash it occurred to the manager that the
very danger he had so lately laughed at was
now upon him. Before he could make a move
to defend himself, the other car swung in front
of his, effectually blocking his progress. Four

men jumped out; the ugly one and the driver who sat on the front seat, and two others, equally unattractive and menacing, from the rear. They swarmed into Ned's car, and working with the savage speed of men used to this sort of thing they pinned the young man's arms to his sides. In spite of his fight and struggles, a bag or cloth was thrown over his head which stifled his first startled cries, and then he was lifted out and carried to the other car.

"Step on it!" Ned heard the other driver command, and in an instant the captive was being driven away. He was a prisoner, he had no doubt, of the League of the Leopard.

"Though I didn't notice that black-bearded fence-flier," thought Ned as he struggled ineffectually to get away from his captors. They held him tight, a man on either side of him on the rear seat of the car. Ned had noted, as the car had swerved past him, that the curtains were up, so he reasoned rightly that he could not be seen by other autoists, the police, or anyone in the streets of Shopton, and consequently there could be no spontaneous attempt to rescue him.

"The Leopard himself wasn't in this kidnapping party," Ned reasoned as he calmed down after his futile effort to escape from the strong hands holding him. "And that little runt of an anarchist wasn't, either. Well, they have me, just as they threatened they would."

It was characteristic of Ned, once the first, natural emotion of fear had passed, to take stock of a situation and to try to figure a way out. This he now did, sitting quietly between his two captors as the car sped onward. The bag over his head was sufficiently porous for him to get some air, but he could see nothing through the folds. He guessed, however, because of the jolting of the car, that he was being driven over a rough, country road.

"They didn't go into Shopton," Ned argued with himself. "They must be taking me to some hiding place out in the suburbs. It was rather foolish of Tom and me not to heed that warning. These men are more desperate than we thought. I should have been on my guard. I only hope they don't get Tom. If they do he can't save me."

That Tom Swift would come to his rescue Ned did not for a moment doubt, and this hopeful idea at once brought to the fore another: the means of letting the young inventor know where he, the captive, was.

"I have my pocket wireless set!" Ned told himself with a feeling of exultation. "These scoundrels don't know that, and as soon as I get a chance I'll send Tom a code signal to come and get me. I only hope they don't search me and take the set away. It's safe now, but——"

Ned felt in his coat pocket, as well as he could

with bound arms, to make sure he had the small but powerful apparatus upon which he planned to rely in just such an emergency as this. It was there, but he was worried for fear it would be taken from him when the time should come for a search.

"I must think up a way to hide it," mused the young manager.

The auto careened along, the road getting rougher and rougher all the while. Finally the car came to a stop after a run of about fifteen minutes, as near as Ned could calculate.

"I think they have brought me about seven miles from where they caught me," reasoned Ned. "My set will work up to ten miles. I can get a signal through to Tom as soon as I'm left alone long enough. Now what's going to happen?" he asked himself half whimsically, though he was far from being in a jovial mood.

"Here's where youse git out, bo," said one of his captors, the voice, tone and words indicating a person of the tramp or hobo species.

"An' no monkey business if youse want t' keep a whole skin," said the man, gripping Ned's left arm.

"You have things your own way now," Ned answered in muffled tones from under the bag. "But you'll get into trouble over this. I have friends who will soon rescue me."

This was pure bluff, but a bluff sometimes

works. However, the two men holding Ned only laughed, and one said:

"Dat Tom Swift'll have t' go some t' git youse out from where we'll hide you. Come on now— scram!"

Ned rightly took this to be an invitation to move, and he preferred to do this rather than to submit to being carried. His arms were bound but his feet were free, and rather stumbling, he managed to get out of the car.

"Now, bo, here are de orders an' see dat youse follers 'em or youse'll git hoit," said one of the captors. "You've got t'climb a ladder, but youse won't git hoited if youse keep on goin'. We ain't goin' t' take de sack offen yer head but we'll loosen yer arms an' all youse'll have t' do will be t' climb de ladder. How about it?"

"I'll climb all right if you'll guarantee I won't be pushed off when I get to the top."

Ned felt himself being led along what seemed to be a cinder path. He tried to judge by the feel of the ground beneath his feet in what part of the country he might be, but it was too much of a riddle. The bag over his head was more tightly drawn. Then his arms were unbound and a voice said:

"One of us is goin' t' climb de ladder ahead of youse, an' one of us'll foller so don't try any funny stunts. Jest climb an' den youse can sit down a while."

It was useless to attempt a fight now, Ned argued. He stretched out his hands and felt them come in contact with the iron rungs of a ladder. Blindfolded, he began to climb upward, hearing the progress of the man ahead of him and the one behind.

"They must be taking me up into some building by way of the fire escape," Ned told himself. He could tell when he passed from the outer air into the more confined space of a room.

Walking cautiously, and placing one foot before the other, Ned found himself walking in darkness across a wooden flooring. The place smelled musty, as if not much fresh air entered.

Suddenly the bag was whisked from his head and Ned, blinking his eyes, saw that he was in a small room with rough wooden walls. Two of the evil-faced men were there grinning at him. A quick glance showed Ned a cot bed, a table and a chair. On the table were some packages of crackers, some canned food and a pitcher of water with a glass.

"Here's where youse'll stay until de boss makes up his mind what t' do wit youse," said the larger of the two evil men. "Youse kin eat dis grub an' dere'll be more when it's gone. We ain't goin' t' starve youse—not yet!" and he chuckled. "Come on!" he called to his companion.

"What about friskin' him?" asked the other as the two were about to leave. For a brief moment they had turned their backs on Ned and this gave him the opportunity he wanted. "He may have a knife or a gat."

"Dat's so!" agreed the big man. "Well, give him de once over!"

The small man passed his hands down Ned's sides, patting his pockets. But the wireless set was now safe up the back of Ned's coat and the garment was so loosely-fitting, being a Norfolk jacket style, that the bulge of the instrument did not show.

"No gat," reported the searcher. "Got a knife, bo?"

Ned willingly handed over his pen knife, thinking it would keep him from being "frisked" further, which it did. For, on receiving what might have been a weapon, the small man said with a grin:

"I guess dat's all. Now youse kin sit down."

"But look here!" began Ned, determined to make one last appeal and to incorporate a threat with it, "you can't leave me here like this. I'll get Tom Swift, the police and the Secret Service men——"

"Can dat spiel!" sneered the large man. "We got youse an' we're goin' t' keep youse. So take it easy!"

There was nothing else for Ned to do. The men went out, locked the door after them, and he was left alone in captivity.

CHAPTER XX

A DIRE THREAT

Tom Swift with Mr. Banlot, the Secret Service man, listened with no little apprehension to the footsteps in the corridor outside the young inventor's laboratory.

"What's getting into Koku?" thought Tom. "Once he allows himself to be drawn away by an imitation cat and now he's let someone get past him."

A moment later, however, Tom's fears vanished as he heard a well-remembered voice saying:

"It's all right, Koku! It's all right! Bless my asparagus tips, but this is a terrible thing to have happen! Ned Newton kidnapped!"

"It's a friend of mine—Mr. Damon," Tom explained to the Secret Service man, and a little later the eccentric individual was in the laboratory listening to all that could be told of Ned's disappearance.

"But Tom, you must get after these scoundrels at once!" declared Mr. Damon. "They must be caught and Ned set free!"

"That's what we're trying to do, Mr. Damon," Tom answered. "We'd be only too glad to rescue Ned, but we don't know where to look for him."

"Bless my fountain pen! I'm going to help you," said Mr. Damon. "That's what I came over to do—offer my services. I came as soon as I heard the bad news. Koku said you had a visitor but I decided this was more important than any caller, so I came on right past your giant, Tom."

"I see you did," and the young inventor smiled slightly. "It's quite all right. Mr. Banlot is helping me on this and I'm trying to help him. But how did you hear that Ned was kidnapped?"

"Oh, it's all over Shopton and Waterfield, too. It's in the papers, that's how I heard."

"You can't keep a thing like this quiet," observed Mr. Banlot.

"I suppose not," Tom agreed. "Well, Mr. Damon, it was good of you to come and offer your help. We may need you. But what will your wife say?"

"Oh, she's all right!" was the quick answer. "She urged me to come."

"She did!" Tom exclaimed, for he knew Mrs. Damon. "Then she didn't mind your going off while she was on her vacation and trying to catch some fish?"

"Not at all," and the odd man laughed.

"How did she like those you bought for her?"

"Say, that was one of the best things I ever did!" said Mr. Damon. "It seems that when my wife came back from her vacation she brought a cat with her. When I got home that night with the fish she thought I'd caught, she was tickled pink when I said the cat could have some. And did he eat—I mean the cat!" chuckled Mr. Damon. "So everything is all right," he concluded.

"I'm glad of that," remarked Tom Swift. "I wish everything were all right in regard to Ned."

"And I wish we could catch that anarchist!" murmured the Secret Service man. "The folks down in Washington are beginning to ask a lot of questions that are hard to answer. I must get that fellow!"

"And I must rescue Ned!" declared Tom. "He ought to be able soon to send me a message."

"Send you a message!" exclaimed Mr. Banlot. "Oh, you mean that the kidnappers will send you a note demanding a ransom or else telling on what terms they'll let your friend go. Is that it?"

"Not exactly," Tom answered. "I hope to hear directly from Ned himself by means of wireless. I'll arrange my receiving set now. Perhaps I should have done it before, but I doubt if Ned would have a chance to get his set working before this."

As he connected the small receiving set he had made so that any signals might be picked up, Tom told his visitors how Ned had arranged a secret code by means of which he hoped to be able to communicate with Tom in case of danger.

"You'd think he had anticipated being kidnapped," remarked Mr. Banlot.

"As a matter of fact, Ned did speak of the possibility that he might be kidnapped," Tom admitted. "But I laughed at it. I saw no reason then for anticipating any such thing. I'm glad now that I helped Ned work out this secret code business."

"Do you think those who kidnapped him will let him send you a message?" asked Mr. Damon.

"Naturally they won't if they know about it," Tom answered. "But Ned may be smart enough to trick them. I hope I may have some word from him soon."

Though they sat and waited in silent apprehension for the clicking and buzzing on Tom's machine which would tell of Ned's effort to send an appeal for help, nothing came through the air. Tom tuned the machine to different short-wave lengths within the range he and Ned had decided upon, but there was no message.

"We may as well start out with the television detector," Tom decided after another hour had passed without a word of news.

"I think so," agreed the Secret Service man. "It's a wonderful machine you have, Tom Swift. It located the Leopard, it may yet pick up the anarchist, and——"

"The best service it could render me would be to find Ned Newton," interrupted Tom.

"Bless my looking glass!" exclaimed Mr. Damon, "I'm sure we shall rescue Ned! Come on, now. Let's go!"

"What about that?" asked Mr. Banlot, pointing to the secret code receiving set.

"We'll take that in the car with us," Tom answered. "I can pick up the signals, if any are sent out while we're moving along, just as radio-equipped police cars get their messages."

"Great!" exclaimed the Secret Service man. "I'll call up one of my men."

With the television detector and the wireless machine in the sedan, which Tom decided on in preference to an open car, the party of four soon set out, for Mr. Banlot's helper had arrived in a short time from the temporary headquarters in Shopton.

"We want to be ready to make a raid on short notice if we can pick up Mr. Newton," said the Secret Service operator.

They went out into the dark and silent night. The search for Ned was not altogether without its objectives, for during the hunt for the Leopard and the anarchist many of the "hide-

outs" of the desperate men with whom these
outlaws associated had been located, either by
Tom Swift or Mr. Banlot and his helpers. One
after another these dens of the criminals were
actually peered into by means of the television
detector. Tom and his friends saw many strange
scenes through brick, stone and wooden walls,
but though they viewed many gangs that doubtless merited arrest, there was no trace of Ned
Newton.

Tom's detector was limited, he admitted, in
that it must be pointed to within forty-five degrees of the object or person which it was desired
to view before becoming effective. This range,
of half a right-angle, made it imperative that the
detector be focused within the two diverging
lines representing this degree of angle before the
radium rays would illuminate the scene.

"I can't scatter my television force in all
directions as can be done on a wireless or ordinary television sending machine," Tom explained. "I'm limited at present, though later I
may be able to make a universal detector that
will take in the whole three hundred and sixty
degrees of a horizon circle."

"Then you can see anything in the world,"
said Mr. Damon.

"Within distance limits, of course," Tom
answered. "But I can't do better than forty-five
degrees now."

This, seemingly, was not enough, for through the weary hours of the night Tom and his friends tried without success to find Ned in captivity. Tired and dispirited, they returned as dawn was breaking, Mr. Banlot and his man going back to their headquarters and Mr. Damon remaining with Tom Swift.

Furthermore, they had not been able to pick up any code signals.

"But we shan't give up!" declared Mr. Damon.

"Indeed not!" Tom assured him.

An intensive search was kept up all the next day and night, not only for Ned but for the Leopard and the anarchist. It was reasoned that these two master-minds among the criminals were responsible for Ned's kidnapping, or more than likely had actually committed it themselves. But the search, aided as it was by Tom Swift's television detector, came to naught.

It was the fifth day since Ned had been kidnapped, and Tom was about to start out with his friends on another phase of the search, when the mail was delivered at his laboratory. Without much interest the young inventor glanced through the pile of letters, but suddenly one attracted his attention. It was most peculiarly addressed by means of letters of the alphabet cut from newspaper advertisements and pasted on the envelope.

"This looks suspicious!" Tom exclaimed to

Mr. Banlot and Mr. Damon. "It may be from the kidnappers."

It was, but they had hidden their identity on the missive in the envelope, for it was also made up of newspaper letters. They formed this dire threat:

"Keep away from us, Tom Swift, with that detector of yours, or your friend Ned Newton will be killed! Lay off from us and we'll clear out. Keep after us and your friend won't be alive much longer. We mean business. League of the Leopard."

On the bottom of the dirty, paste-encrusted sheet of paper were three yellow thumb marks.

CHAPTER XXI

TOM SWIFT DECIDES

With horror showing on their faces, the three looked at the sinister warning. That it was no joke, or the work of some crank, was evidenced by the Leopard's spots.

"Are they the same as the others?" asked Mr. Banlot, pointing to the three yellow smears.

"We can soon tell," Tom answered.

With a large reading glass he and his friends compared the latest marks of the Leopard with those known to have been left by the black-bearded man. They tallied in every respect.

"This is from Ned's kidnappers all right," Tom declared. "There can be no doubt of that."

"They've taken precautions against any hand-writing being traced," said Mr. Banlot, "but they don't seem to think we have the finger, or rather thumb prints."

"That won't do us much good unless we catch the Leopard himself, and perhaps this anarchist you're after, Mr. Banlot," said Tom.

"I suppose not! I never was so beaten before! These rats have me completely fooled!" said the Secret Service man. "My reputation is at stake. I must get them!"

"And Ned's life seems to be at stake," spoke Tom quietly, but with intense feeling. "We must consider that."

"Of course," agreed Mr. Banlot. "They have us buffaloed, Tom Swift. What are you going to do?"

For the moment the young inventor did not reply. He sat down at his desk, looked first at the television detector waiting to be used; then to the wireless set, waiting for a message from Ned; and thence to the threatening missive with the Leopard's sinister spots standing out on it.

"Bless my baked potato!" exclaimed Mr. Damon. "These scoundrels ought to be shot, hanged, electrocuted or whatever the legal penalty is in this state for such a crime. I'll help inflict the penalty myself. I surely will!"

"First we have to catch them," reminded Mr. Banlot.

"That's right!" said Tom. "And we shall!"

"Do you realize what your decision means?"

"Fully," replied Tom.

"They say, in effect, in this note," went on Mr. Banlot, picking it up to scan it more closely, "that if you will let them alone and not try to discover them with your wonderful detector, Tom Swift, they will release your friend."

"I understand that, Mr. Banlot."

"But if you keep on their trail he will be killed."

"I'm going to keep after them!" cried Tom Swift in a ringing voice. "Ned must take his chance. It's just what he would tell me to do if he were here. It's like a problem in algebra. On one side is the life of the best friend I have in the world," and Tom's voice broke a little. Then he went on, "On the other side is the welfare of my country. I'm not being heroic or anything like that, but these criminals must be wiped off the earth. They can't be allowed to go on. What's my life—what's Ned's life—compared to the safety of our country? I know some things you gentlemen don't know," Tom said more quietly as he thought of his secret gas formula. "If we give in to these rats now, we'll have them at our throats again soon. They must be caught and I'm going to keep after them. Ned will have to take his chance. It's just what he would want me to do!"

Then, having made his decision, Tom Swift turned aside, walked to the window with blinking eyes and blew his nose very hard, a most unheroic proceeding. There was a moment of strained silence. Then Mr. Damon burst out with:

"Bless my—bless my—dash it all, Tom, I don't know what in the world to say, except I'm with you on this and we'll—we'll smash those

scoundrels into—bless my talcum powder! Bless
my handkerchief! I believe I'm catching cold!"
And Mr. Damon blew his nose very hard.

"It's what I expected of you, Mr. Swift," said
the Secret Service man quietly. "But it's going
to be—terribly hard!"

"Come on!" Tom exclaimed, turning back
from the window, his emotions now under control. "We'll start after these fellows at once!
We'll try again!"

"I'm going to telephone Washington to send
us some more men!" cried Mr. Banlot. "We'll
wipe these scoundrels off the earth!"

When, with the television detector and the
wireless receiving set in their sedan, Tom and
his friends started out on the search again that
morning, Ned Newton was still a captive. The
days that had passed since his kidnapping had
been weary days. The nights had been long
nights, but he had not given up hope.

His first action, after having been left alone
in the little room, was to take stock of his pre-
dicament. He was a prisoner but with food and
water within reach, and there was a little light
and air coming from a small window high up on
what he took to be the rear wall of his place of
captivity.

It was this rear wall that first attracted Ned's
curious attention, for it was different from the
other walls of his prison cell. Three sides of his

place of captivity were made of heavy planks. The fourth side, which Ned called the back, was in the form of a wide curve and the boards were narrow and more closely fitted than those on the other three sides.

"This is a queer place," mused Ned. "It's some sort of a building, or part of a building, and I'm rather high up. That's plain, for I had to climb a ladder to get here. But this back wall is most peculiar. I wonder what sort of a place they have me in?"

He had nothing with which he might try to effect his escape. His knife had been taken from him and there was no tool in the room. However, he still had his wireless set. He took it from the back of his coat and hid it in the bed which, he was glad to note, was clean. He took stock of the food, calculating there would be enough for several days, and then he drank some of the water.

"As soon as I think they've gone away for a while I'll try sending out a code message," Ned mused. He waited and listened. There was no sound save the distant whistling of locomotives, upon hearing which Ned argued that he was not far from the railroad.

He tried to force the door, but it was solid, and firmly locked. There was no way of making an opening in any of the stout, wooden walls. Then Ned sat down, tried to reason things out, gave that up as a bad job, and began sending out his secret code signals. There was no electric outlet in his prison, although there was an oil lantern which he judged would give him light at night. He had no means of power save in the small storage battery of his little set.

"That will have to do," Ned reasoned. "I could send out stronger signals if I could hook this up to an electric light socket but there's no chance of that now. Well, here goes!"

He began tapping out in the secret code the words:

"Blime zax fernmo apentish wacko lushford."

"I am in trouble—help me."

But Tom Swift never heard them.

CHAPTER XXII

THE CODE MESSAGE

DAY after day, night after night, Ned Newton remained a prisoner of the men from the League of the Leopard. Day after day, night after night he sent out the code message which he and Tom had agreed upon, but no help came. Then Ned, whose nerves were beginning to give way under the strain, examined his set and found that the little dry cell storage battery had gone dead.

"I can't get the signals out!" he exclaimed. "I can't get word to Tom! No wonder he doesn't come to rescue me! What am I going to do?"

Rendered desperate by his plight, Ned resolved upon a bold stroke. The light in his room consisted of a railroad man's lantern of the type in which the glass is protected against breakage by a wide mesh of heavy wire.

"I'll bend off some of that wire," Ned decided, "and see if I can't make some sort of a hook to pick the lock of the door."

He began this at once. It was hard work to bend the heavy wire back and forth until it broke, but at last he did it. Laboriously he fashioned a sort of hook and was trying to pick the lock with this, when one afternoon the door was suddenly opened and he was confronted with the larger of the two evil men who had brought him to this strange prison.

"Ah, so dat's de game, is it?" cried the fellow. "Well, we'll put a stop to dat. Youse can't have any light. Here, take dis lantern out," he told his shorter companion.

"Why can't I have any light?" asked Ned, who was much disappointed by his lock-picking failure. At the same time he berated himself, as he had not ceased to do since he found the battery dead, for his careless oversight.

"Youse kin have a light," the big rough answered as the smaller man took away the lantern minus the wire guard. Ned's piece of wire was also confiscated. "But it'll be a light youse can't open any doors wit," jeered the guard. "Tell Fatty t' come here wit his tools an' some wire," was the next order to the short man.

Ned was all attention at the mention of the word "wire." He thought he might get another piece that would enable him to pick the lock on the door, which was of heavy though simple construction. Ned could not imagine what the wire was wanted for.

"Unless they're going to wire me up tight," he thought with a sudden sinking of the heart.

He soon discovered what the plans of his captors were. A big, blowsy tramp of a man, whom the name "Fatty" perfectly fitted, slouched in with some tools and a coil of flexible, incandescent electric light wire cord on his arm.

"We's goin' t' light youse up in style!" jeered the big guard who had not left the room.

Ned could scarcely believe that an electric light was to be put in his prison. Yet such was the case, and at once his heart started beating madly, for now he saw a way to send Tom that code signal. The pocket wireless set he still had could be operated either from its own dry cell or from an incandescent light socket, there being a resistance coil in the apparatus to shunt off most of the current, only a small amount being needed for the short waves.

"This will work better than the dry cell," mused Ned as he watched Fatty at work. "I'm in luck!" He glanced around his cheerless prison and hoped he would soon be taken from it.

Aside from being kept a prisoner, Ned Newton had not been harshly treated by his captors. He had been given plenty of plain food, mostly of the canned variety, he had plenty of water to drink and some to wash with, and even a towel and soap had been provided, though the latter was of the brown, laundry kind.

Aside from the two guards and now Fatty, Ned had seen none of his captors since the day he was kidnapped from his car. He had had no glimpse of the Leopard or the little anarchist. The latter he had never seen so he had to rely on Mr. Banlot's description.

"He may be in this building, whatever it is," thought Ned, who had not been able to discover where he was nor the character of his prison. The small but heavy upright boards on the back of his cell were still a puzzle to him. "I guess both the Leopard and the anarchist are around here," thought Ned. "They're keeping out of my way and they let others of the gang do their dirty work. But if I can hook my set into the light socket I'll send word to Tom."

It was evident that Fatty, though now a tramp, had once been an electrical worker. In a short time he had run a wire in from some point outside Ned's cell and fastened it to the ceiling, letting a length hang down. On the end of this extension a tin-shaded, incandescent bulb was screwed into a regulation socket, and the big guard said:

"Dere's yer light. Youse can't open any doors wit dat!"

"Not unless he has an electric drill!" chuckled Fatty.

"An' he ain't got dat—not even a knife!" sneered the guard. "De boss'll be in t' see youse t' day," he added as he and Fatty left.

Had it not been for the confidence he had in

his wireless set Ned would have been as gloomy as ever after the two went out. For a moment he had hoped, after sensing what was going on, that some opening might be left in the door through which the wire was strung so that he could enlarge it and get out. But Fatty bored only a small hole high up in the wall and ran his wire through that.

"A fly couldn't crawl through," Ned reflected, "but now I can signal Tom. He must have been waiting for a code message all this while, and I couldn't get it to him, though I thought it was going out. So the boss is coming, eh? The Leopard, I suppose."

Ned was much puzzled as to the location of his prison and its character. He wanted to know something about it so that he might give Tom a clue.

"Maybe I can get it out of the Leopard when he comes," he thought.

Ned knew that he must be in some large building for he could hear dim and distant echoes of persons above, below, on either side, and in front of him at times. From the rear the only sounds he heard were those made by passing trains, the whistling engines of which often sounded in the night. Yet the railroad was not very close, Ned argued, or the sounds would have been plainer.

"About all I can tell Tom is that I'm not more than a mile from some railroad," Ned reasoned.

"I'm in a building with some sort of ladder on the outside—a fire escape, maybe."

Ned knew that this was a very vague direction to wireless to Tom, but there was no help for it.

"He may be able to pick me up in the television detector," Ned told himself. "I'm glad he perfected it before I was kidnapped. But what a sap I was not to be sure my battery was alive! Well, I've the real juice now."

Ned decided to wait until after dark to attach the set to the wire in his cell. He wondered how it was that this gang of tramps and outlaws could command an electric light circuit.

"Maybe they tapped the wires in the street or along some road and are stealing the current," Ned reasoned.

With his next meal came the Leopard. The same big, black-bearded foreigner whom Ned had seen in the Swift yard under such dramatic circumstances entered the cell soon after the big guard set down Ned's tray of food.

"So, you are here!" sneered the Leopard, sitting on Ned's cot which sagged with his weight. "Well, it will not be long now." He spoke with a strange, clipped accent to his words but seemed to be a man of education.

"What do you mean? Where am I, anyhow?" Ned demanded.

"That's for you to find out!" chuckled the

man who wore around his neck on a chain a small brass plate on which a leopard was stamped. "But you will not be here long."

"Then you are going to let me go?" asked Ned hopefully.

"You shall be *sent* out—not allowed to go— and you will be sent to your death!" snarled the foreigner.

Ned started suddenly, for his nerves were under none too good control since his captivity.

"Death!" he faltered. "You won't dare kill me! My friends will soon be here to rescue me!"

"Ha! Ha!" laughed the Leopard. "So they think! So you think! But it has been many days since Tom Swift started to look for you with that spying television detector of his. That machine will soon be mine along with other secrets. You need not count on being rescued, though if Tom Swift does as he has been told to do you may soon be free to go to him."

"What do you mean?" asked Ned.

"Word has been sent to him that unless he ceases trying to discover me and my friends," said the Leopard in a voice that was like a snarl, "your life will pay the penalty. He has but two days more. If he does not give up his activities with that detector and cease from trying to help the Secret Service men, you will be killed. That message has gone to Tom Swift, and the League of the Leopard does what it threatens to do."

He touched the image of the beast hanging around his neck and bared his teeth in a sinister smile, twining his fingers in his black beard as though it might contain a nest of serpents.

So that, perhaps, was why Tom had not come to the rescue. He had to make his choice between serving the interests of his country and saving the life of his chum.

"But if I know Tom Swift," Ned reasoned, "and I think I do, he won't let that threat stand in the way. He'll defy these rats and keep after them. And I'm going to show them I'm not afraid."

Then Ned stood up, and in furious, hot words told the sinister Leopard that he was not afraid to die, that he knew Tom would not cease in his efforts to track down the gang, that the federal men would never allow themselves to be intimidated, and that within a short time the place of Ned's imprisonment would be raided by the authorities and the Leopard and his whelps sent to jail.

"So!" exclaimed the big, black-bearded man, when Ned, trembling with justifiable rage and sweating from his fiery speech, had sunk into the chair. "You are brave at any rate, young man, thus to defy the Leopard League. I give you credit for that. But do not hope for too much! We have great power and Tom Swift will think twice before defying us and continuing on our trail when he has been told it will mean your death. He will never save you!"

"Yes, he will!" cried Ned. "He'll be here soon, and even if he doesn't come I'd rather die than live, knowing that by so doing I had helped you and your dirty gang of outlaws! Now get out!"

Afterward Ned wondered how he had had the nerve to thus order the Leopard from the cell, but he did, and strange as it may seem the big foreigner left with a look of admiration at Ned.

"I almost wish I had such a young man as you with me!" he murmured. "You are brave—yes, very brave!"

"It doesn't take much to be brave before swine like you!" snapped Ned. For a moment a dangerous light shone in the eyes of the Leopard. Then, with a shrug of his massive shoulders he went out, murmuring:

"The cause—the cause above everything!"

The big guard looked in, leered at Ned, then locked the door.

Ned was not hungry. His emotional outburst had taken away his appetite. The cell grew dark, so he turned on the incandescent lamp and it glowed almost cheerily in his lonely prison.

"I have the juice!" Ned exclaimed. "And now for the code message!"

He plugged in his set and in the darkness began to transmit the message.

"Blime zax fernmo apentish wacko lushford."
"I am in trouble—help me."

Over and over again he sent this out, adding at times the best description he could formulate about his prison.

"Will Tom get this?" Ned mused. "I'm sure the signals are going out now. But will he listen after having received none in so long a time? If he gets the message, will he come to rescue me?"

Ned thought of what the Leopard had said. Tom had been told to cease all efforts to locate the criminals, or forfeit the life of his friend. With renewed hope in his heart, however, Ned went on sending the message:

"I am in trouble—help me."

CHAPTER XXIII

THE WATER TOWER

Defying by his actions the League of the Leopard and all persons connected with it, Tom Swift, far from ceasing to search out the criminals and rescue Ned, redoubled his efforts. Starting out the very day the sinister warning about Ned's death was received, the young inventor, Mr. Damon and the Secret Service man intensified their search.

One of the first places the television detector had been turned on was of course the crystal cave where the Leopard had been seen in possession of the gas secret. As might have been expected, since the raid on the place, the outlaws had given the cave a wide berth. The television machine showed no one within the cavern save some curious boys drawn thither by the newspaper stories.

"The Leopard won't go back there," Mr. Banlot gave as his opinion.

"I suppose not," Tom agreed. "But we didn't dare pass it up."

Again that day and again that night other

known haunts and dens of the criminals were visited; that is, the television machine was focused on them. There was no sign of Ned Newton. Neither was the Leopard located nor the dangerous anarchist.

"We have them worried," declared Mr. Banlot. "I have reports from several distant places that the men who are known to have been in communication with Kalhofski are keeping well under cover. They are afraid of you and of your television detector, Tom Swift."

"I hope they are afraid enough not to injure Ned," was the answer. "But I know he wouldn't want me to stop even to save him!"

"The rats!" snapped the Secret Service man. "If they harm him it will go hard with them when at last we catch them!"

"If we can only locate them before they touch Ned!" murmured Tom over and over again.

So the search went on by night and by day as before. Additional men came from Washington but they were all at a loss to know how to proceed. The Leopard and his whelps seemed to have hidden themselves deep in the earth in some secret lair that even the television detector could not locate.

"It's only because we don't know just where to aim it," Tom said after several failures. "If I could only get a clue and could focus on a point within forty-five degrees of Ned's prison I'd soon have him out. If I could only get some word from him!"

"Why doesn't he work that wireless he has?" asked Mr. Banlot.

"I can't understand Ned's failure to send me a code message," Tom answered. "More than likely the men who kidnapped him have found the set on him and have taken it away. I'm afraid it's useless now to hope for a message."

Tom listened in, however, several times each day and night, hoping against hope. Meanwhile the several agencies at work had had no success in locating the kidnappers or the other criminals.

A full week had passed since Ned had become a prisoner. It was the night when the electric current was first available to the prisoner that Tom Swift, Mr. Damon, Mr. Banlot and another Secret Service operator were out in the big sedan with the television detector and the wireless set.

The searchers had been to several of the suspected places and to some new haunts where, it was reported, strange men were congregating. Looking into these dens of iniquity by means of his strange machine, Tom saw many dangerous characters, but none of them was the Leopard, none of them was the anarchist, and none of them was the kidnapped prisoner.

It was now midnight. After a visit to a suspected shack, Tom, weary and discouraged, decided to go back home. The car was turned in the direction of Shopton, and hardly had the turn been made, when a signal was heard on the wireless receiving apparatus. At first it seemed to be only a faint buzz or clicking.

"Bless my shoe laces!" exclaimed Mr. Damon who sat near it. "What's that, Tom?"

"Some signal," Tom answered. "It may be only induction from the car generator, but——" He ceased speaking and began to manipulate the knobs of the dials. The buzzing and clicking became louder and then there issued faintly but clearly on the night air dots, dashes and spaces in the Morse code.

"It's Ned! It's Ned!" cried Tom. "He's got his set working at last! He's sending me the secret code! Quiet, everybody, please!"

Breathlessly Tom and the others listened. Mr. Banlot was the only other person in the car besides Tom Swift who could translate the Morse dots, dashes and spaces into words.

"Blime zax fernmo apentish wacko lushford," repeated the Secret Service man. "That doesn't make any sense. He must have his machine twisted."

"It's code!" exclaimed Tom, greatly excited. "It's the secret code we made up between us. At last I'm in communication with Ned."

"Where is he?" demanded Mr. Damon.

"I don't know yet. I'll find out, though, as

soon as I let him know I have his message. Now we'll get those kidnappers!"

Quickly Tom switched his set from receiving to sending and sent word to Ned, whose whereabouts at this time could not be determined, that his message had been received.

"We'll come to you soon," Tom sent in code to his chum. "I'm going to the laboratory now. Allow me half an hour to arrive there. Then send another message and let us know just where you are. We'll come to your rescue."

Tom waited for an acknowledgment from Ned, which soon arrived. The prisoner added that he was well, had enough to eat and spoke of the threat of death, adding:

"You'd better make it snappy, Tom!"

"I will!" answered the young inventor. "I can get your messages better in the laboratory, and since you don't know where you are, I'll have to listen from two different points and locate your prison by triangular computation. We'll soon have you out!"

All speed was made back to the laboratory and there Tom set up a more efficient wireless set for receiving word from Ned and communicating with him. The half hour stipulated by the young inventor was not yet up before Ned was again sending his code signals.

Anxiously Tom listened, translating for the benefit of Mr. Damon. Quickly Ned told him what had happened to him and described the appearance of his prison as best he could. This best was none too good, however, owing to the fact that he had been taken to it blindfolded.

"The back wall of the room I am in is made of small, upright boards," Ned wirelessed to Tom. "It looks as if this building had once been a big tank."

This was a puzzle to all of them. They could recall no such structure in the neighborhood, and it was certain, from the strength of Ned's signals, that he was only about seven miles from them.

"In effect, then," said Mr. Banlot, "we have to search over a circle seven miles in diameter."

"Seven miles in radius," corrected Tom. "We are the center of the circle and Ned is a prisoner in some direction from here about seven miles away. But we won't have to do all that work."

"What, then?" asked Mr. Damon.

"I can get one direction by picking up Ned's signals here in the laboratory," Tom explained. "If I go some distance from here and get the signals coming in from another direction, all I'll have to do will be to draw two converging lines. Where the lines meet will be the place where Ned is held."

"Bless my trigonometry!" cried the odd man. "Do that, Tom Swift, and let's rescue him and catch those rats!"

Another message was sent to Ned bidding him to keep up his courage and to send more code signals in half an hour. By that time Tom could reach a distant point to pick them up, since the converging lines of messages must be separated by a considerable distance at the receiving end to insure proper intersection at the point from which Ned was sending them.

The second code signal was received from the captive. It was short and to the point.

"I had to stop sending. The Leopard was just in my cell and he said you had until tomorrow night to quit, Tom, or I'd be killed. But don't quit! There's a bad gang here. I had a glimpse of one man who is the anarchist Mr. Banlot wants, I'm sure."

"Oh, if I can only get him!" exclaimed the Secret Service man as Tom translated this for him. "Can you locate the place where they are holding Ned?"

Tom had a road map of the country around Shopton. Under the dome light of the sedan car this chart was now consulted and on it Tom drew two lines, one from his laboratory, the other from the point where they had received Ned's last message. The lines met and crossed near a lonely section of the country not far from where Mr. Damon lived.

"There's a railroad near there," Tom said, looking at the map, "but nothing else that I know of. I haven't been in that section of late, but I can't recall any building that would serve as a headquarters for these bandits or as a prison for Ned."

"Let me look at the map," suggested Mr. Damon. When he had scanned it he uttered a cry of surprise.

"What is it?" demanded Tom.

"It's the water tower!" exclaimed the odd man. "Bless my bathtub, Tom Swift, they must have made a hang-out in the old place, those rats! And that's where Ned is. Quick! We must go to the old water tower!"

CHAPTER XXIV

CLOSING IN

Just for a moment Tom and Mr. Banlot thought, because of Mr. Damon's excited manner and his strange words, that the strain had been too much for the odd gentleman. However, though Mr. Damon was acting queerly, he seemed to know what he was talking about and there was a steady look in his eyes.

"What do you mean—water tower?" asked Tom. "Not even this gang can live inside a tank of water, and if they'd drowned Ned there——"

"He can't be drowned, you know," spoke the Secret Service man. "You just heard from him and he's all right."

"That's so," Tom admitted. "But what do you mean about a water tower, Mr. Damon? No one can live in a tank filled with water."

"Not when there's water in it," chuckled the odd man. "But if the tank happens to be *empty* it would make a good hiding place and that's where the Leopard and the anarchist have Ned, I'm sure of it. Look, the railroad used to run right past here."

Mr. Damon traced the line on the map. Then Tom remembered.

"A few years ago," went on Mr. Damon, "the company straightened out a sharp curve and ran the railroad tracks this way." Again he indicated on the map before he proceeded. "That left an old water tower without any further use as far as the railroad was concerned. It was a big tank raised on a supporting platform, and the engines used to stop there to get water for their boilers. I haven't any doubt but that this gang has taken over the old tank, fitted up rooms in it and made it their headquarters. And that's where they have Ned a prisoner!"

"I believe he's right!" said Mr. Banlot.

"I begin to understand now," Tom said. "This would explain what Ned told me in code about being made to climb some sort of outside iron ladder. He thought it might be a fire escape."

"There's an iron ladder leading up outside the old water tower," said Mr. Damon. "I often drive past it and I've noticed it. Part of the ladder leads up to the very top so that men could clean out the filling pipe, I suppose. But it would be easy for those scoundrels to change the ladder to enable them to climb up it and enter the bottom of the tank through a hole or trap door cut in it. I believe that's just what they did and they've been hiding there ever since you chased them out of the crystal cave, Tom!"

"It may be so. It fits in with everything else so far. The old water tower! An ideal hiding place! Well, now we have something like a clue. How far is it from here?"

"About seven miles," Mr. Damon reported.

"That also tallies with Ned's signals," Tom stated. "Well, I begin to have some hope now."

"Yes! It's the best lead yet!" exclaimed Mr. Banlot. "I only trust we aren't too late!"

"What do you mean?" asked Tom.

"Well, you recall they threatened to kill Ned if you didn't stop trailing them. They may not go as far as that," said Mr. Banlot, "but they may injure him. They are a terrible gang. We'll have to work sharply to beat them."

"We'll close in on them at once!" Tom decided. "We can go to this water tower and see if Ned is inside. If he is we'll raid the place at once."

"No, we can't do that. There aren't enough of us," said Mr. Banlot. "We'll need more help. A big, empty water tank standing on a framework twenty feet or more from the ground is an awkward place to raid. We shall have to make careful plans."

"Get a machine gun and some cannon and raze the place!" suggested Mr. Damon.

"And maybe injure Ned!" Tom exclaimed. "No, we can't do that. As Mr. Banlot says, we'll have to make careful plans."

"At least we can send Ned a message that we know where he is and that we're going to rescue him, can't we, Tom?"

"Oh, yes," was the answer. "And we'll turn the television detector on him in the tank. At least we can see him tonight!"

"And tomorrow we'll raid those rats!" snapped Mr. Banlot.

More heartened now than at any time since the kidnapping of Ned Newton, Tom and his friends drove in the car toward the old water tower. They proceeded cautiously as they neared the place and did not go too close, for they surmised there would be guards and sentinels on the lookout.

"There it is!" said Mr. Damon as the old tank became visible against the horizon of the sky dimly lit by moonlight. "That's it! That's where Ned is!"

As well as they could they observed the water tower from a secluded highway near the old railroad. There was no sign of life about the abandoned structure, not even a gleam of light.

Being so close, Tom did not dare send Ned another radio code message for fear the noise of the sending apparatus in the car would be heard by possible scouts or sentinels.

"We can use the television detector and make sure he is in there," said the young inventor. "I can turn that on. It's silent."

Quickly the clever apparatus was connected, switched on, and the radium projector and vision lens focused on the water tower about a quarter of a mile away. Tom took the first view, moving the lens to take in by degrees the old tank from top to bottom.

Like powerful but invisible X-rays, the television electrons penetrated the thick wooden walls of the water tower. Tom saw, and the others in their turn also discovered that the structure had been divided into rooms by rough board partitions. The place now had two separate floors or stories. The top one consisted of several bunk quarters where Tom could see many rough men stretched out, some asleep, others reclining, talking or playing cards. In a small, walled-off space on the lower floor Tom found what he wanted.

"There's Ned!" cried the young inventor. "I can see him! He's alive and safe yet—all alone in a sort of cell. He's lying on a cot waiting for us to rescue him!"

"Bless my telescope!" cried Mr. Damon. "Let me have a look!"

They all saw Ned a captive almost as plainly as if they were in the water tower prison with him, though the image was, of course, reduced in size.

"Is the anarchist there?" asked Mr. Banlot.

"I haven't seen him yet," Tom answered, "nor

the Leopard. But they may be in another part of the tank. I've focused on only Ned's prison so far."

He made an adjustment of the apparatus, took a look through the visor hood and tensely exclaimed:

"There they both are! The Leopard and the anarchist!"

"Then we have them, the rats!" murmured the Secret Service man. "We'll close in on them within a few hours."

CHAPTER XXV

THE RESCUE

SNAPPY, intensive work, imperative telephone messages and rapid arming against desperate men occupied the next few hours of what remained of the night. Speeding back to his shop, Tom sent Ned a secret code message, telling him to be on the watch for the rescue party shortly before dawn.

"It will be the best time to catch those scoundrels off guard," Mr. Banlot had said.

"If we approach openly, in force," objected Tom, who was fearful for Ned's safety, "they may take alarm and do something desperate."

"We'll have to use strategy," said the Secret Service man. "Leave this to me. Put on your oldest, most ragged clothes, and you too, Mr. Damon. Tom, I suppose you'll want Koku to come along?"

"Oh, certainly."

"Then have him dress as nearly as he can like a railroad track laborer. That's how my men and I will disguise ourselves."

"What's the idea?" asked Tom.

"We'll approach that water tower in squads of a few at a time, made up to look as if we were workmen come to tear it down. I've learned that this is the intention of the railroad company, for the officials have heard the place is a rendezvous for tramps, if not a worse element. It will seem natural for a gang of laborers to converge on the tank to demolish it. Doubtless the inmates have heard this is to be done sooner or later and they won't be surprised.

"They may object and parley with us, but that's just what I want. It will give us a chance to get close and then we'll rush the place and save Ned."

Tom admitted that the plan was a good one. It was not long before he and Mr. Damon, with Koku and two strong men from the shop, all wearing old and ragged clothes, were in the auto driving toward the water tower. Eradicate pleaded to be one of the rescue party but Tom had to tell the faithful old Negro that he was needed to help guard the shop. So Eradicate did not mind Koku's mocking smile as the giant went off.

Other cars containing purposely ragged and disreputable looking Secret Service men started out at the same time as Tom's party and headed for the objective but by a different route. Tom stopped his machine in a secluded place and took another look through the television detector. He saw Ned dozing on his cot. The Leopard and the anarchist were asleep in an adjoining room.

"It won't be long now," Tom said softly as he and his friends alighted for the walk to the tank. It would be risky to bring the cars too near.

Dawn was just reddening the sky when the ragged men, ostensibly railroad workers, converged on the water tower. Tom and Koku, with Mr. Damon and Mr. Banlot, were in the front rank. They reached the iron ladder which, as surmised, led to a trap door in the bottom of the tank.

"I hope it isn't fastened," said Mr. Banlot, who claimed the right to be the first to ascend. He had the authority of Uncle Sam back of him and ahead of him was an ugly automatic. "A trap door is an awkward thing to open when standing on a ladder if there is someone on top of the other side of it," he told Tom, "but I'm counting on it being open. These rats don't suspect anything, I believe."

Mr. Banlot climbed the iron rungs, followed by Tom and then by Koku. The rungs sagged under the giant's weight but held safely.

"It's open!" the Secret Service man whispered down as he pushed up the trap door. "We've caught 'em! I think they're all asleep! Come on as quietly as you can!"

One after another of the raiding party climbed up into the old water tower. It was a desperate move. A sudden rush on the part of the reckless men inside and all of the invaders might be killed. But luck was with them. As the last of the Secret Service men got into the tank, something roused the big man who had helped guard Ned. He came blinking out of a room, one of several built on radii from the centre of the tank.

"Wot's dis? Wot's dis? Who are youse?"

"Federal men!" snapped Mr. Banlot. "You're under arrest! Hands up!" and he covered the fellow with the automatic, but not before the guard had let out a warning yell of:

"We're raided! Scram, everybody!"

There was no place whither the scoundrels could escape. There was but one entrance to the tank and that was securely held.

"Scatter, boys, and round 'em up!" commanded Mr. Banlot.

Up the rude stairs leading to the second floor rushed the federal men. Tom and Mr. Damon together with Koku, made for Ned's prison, the location of which they were familiar with from having viewed it through the television detector. Koku carried an iron bar and one blow of this demolished the lock. Into Ned's cell rushed his friends.

"What is it? What is it?" cried the young

manager confusedly, awakened from his sleep.

"We've come to save you, Ned!" cried Tom Swift. "Your code message worked fine!"

"Not any better than your detector, I guess. Gosh, old man, but I'm glad you got here!" said Ned. "I began to think it was all up with me."

"You knew I'd come, didn't you?"

"Yes, but after that ultimatum——"

"As if that would stop me! Well, it's all over now!"

"Not yet!" cried a loud, rasping, snarling voice at the door. "You aren't out of here yet. I told you what I'd do, Tom Swift, and——"

It was the Leopard! His black beard bristling, his clothes awry, his eyes seeming to snap fire, he rushed at Tom and Ned. But Koku stepped forward. There was a blow from the iron bar and the Leopard went down and stayed down.

"Him no more blow smoke in Koku's nose!" said the giant, smiling expansively.

Several shots were heard in distant parts of the tank; shots, yells and cries for mercy. But the Federal men had no mercy on such as these —desperate men who would tear apart a country which they dishonored by their presence.

With the head of the League of the Leopard a prisoner, the other whelps quickly surrendered. Some had been wounded, one fatally, and two of the Federal men had been slightly hurt by shots. The Leopard had had all the fight taken out of him by Koku's blow, and when he recovered his senses he found himself securely bound.

Then into Ned's cell, which was made a sort of headquarters, came Mr. Banlot, leading a small, cringing man with a red beard and a scar on his face.

"I have him!" exclaimed the Secret Service agent. "Kalhofski!"

"Is that the dangerous anarchist?" exclaimed Tom in some surprise.

"He's more dangerous than he looks, not so much physically as mentally. But he's done for now. He'll go back where he came from."

"Don't send me back! They'll kill me!" whined the fellow.

"A good job if they did!" said a Federal man who was nursing a bullet-wounded hand. "He's the rat who shot me before I could clip him."

The battle was soon over. One by one the bound prisoners were lowered through the trap door and put into the cars of the Secret Service men to be taken safely to jail. Tom took Ned home with him and there was great rejoicing in the Swift house a little later. Tom's wife telephoned the good news to Helen Morton and she came over to breakfast with the now merry party. Tom told what he and his friends had done to rescue Ned and the latter described all that had happened to him.

"We must go to see this Leopard in jail and

find out what his game was," Tom decided. "I guess the Federal men will help us get a confession out of him in return for our helping them locate Kalhofski."

"Indeed we will," Mr. Banlot agreed when, a few days later, Tom expressed his wish. "Metomsix, or the Leopard, will own up. He's scared out of his life. That blow of your giant's settled him. His fighting spirit is broken."

In his halting confession the Leopard told almost everything that Tom Swift wanted to know. He and the anarchist had nothing in common except that they were both against organized governments. So, meeting by chance, they had thrown their fortunes together and with their deluded human tools had congregated first in one place and then in another, when they were finally driven out by Tom's relentless television detector.

Argad Metomsix, to give the Leopard one of his names, admitted that he knew he and his cohorts could not be safe from the penetrating rays of the television machine. That was why Ned had been kidnapped, his life being held over Tom's head as a threat. But the scheme had failed.

The Leopard League, a fantastic group of dangerous men had been cleverly conceived by the black-bearded ruffian, who was a highly educated foreigner. His egotistical, warped brain had gone wrong. He knew Korbis Alhazar, the inventor of the secret gas formula which Tom had purchased in the name of humanity. Visiting the inventor shortly before the latter's death, the Leopard had forced the old chemist, by threats of bodily harm, to reveal to whom he had sold the secret.

Thus, learning about Tom Swift, the Leopard had determined to get possession of the dangerous formula. He had come to America on a forged passport, as the anarchist had done, and then had begun to lay his plans.

The Leopard had set himself to spy systematically upon the Swift plant. This was shortly after the secret vault had been finished when Tom had no idea that there was danger in his ownership of the gas secret. Moreover, the Leopard was on his trail. Why the League of the Leopard was so named, the head of the organization never divulged. Doubtless any ruthless beast would have served as a symbol.

When his secret vault was finished and the gas formula and other valuable plans had been stored underground, Tom did not establish the precautions he later put into practice of having his laboratory guarded. One night, after many failures, the Leopard entered the yard of the Swift plant. Spying, he saw through a window how Tom removed the picture and started the mechanism that opened the concealed stairs.

The Leopard was an expert mechanic and locksmith. Having learned the location of the vault he bided his time and one night, when the place was deserted, entered the laboratory, descended the stairs, made his way into the vault and departed with the box containing the formula. But he was afraid to smash the box with the papers, after reading the Latin warning, thinking, he said (as Tom had guessed), there might be a bomb inside that would destroy the secret and himself unless the opening was made in the regular way. This he failed to discover but might have if given more time. However, Tom recovered the formula and cheated the Leopard. After thus being balked, the dangerous foreigner determined upon bolder measures in fighting Tom. But the television detector was too much for him and his band.

What the Leopard intended to do with the formula Tom could not get him to say. That the outlaw intended the destruction of some nation, or perhaps nations, he could not doubt.

"Will you tell me one thing more?" Tom asked when the sordid confession was almost over.

"If it does not betray my plans, yes," was the answer. "For I warn you, I warn you all, that some day I shall succeed. The world is wrong! I shall make it over and make it right!"

"How did you get over my high fence?" asked

Tom. "My manager says you came flying at him, but that's impossible."

"I did in a manner, yes," was the answer. "In my own country I was once champion pole vaulter," went on the Leopard with the first and only real smile ever seen on his grim, ugly face. "I had a long pole and I vaulted the fence with it. Sixteen feet was my record, and your fence is but fifteen. That's how I twisted my foot—pole-vaulting in my own country years ago."

"How did you get back over the fence?" asked Tom, knowing that vaulters always let go the pole on the side of the bar from which they leap, and the fence in this case might be likened to a bar.

"I had a long leather thong attached to the top of the pole and tied around my wrist. When I landed on the inside of the fence I pulled the pole over and leaped back when I got ready."

"Whew!" exclaimed Ned, who admitted that this was probably the solution of the puzzle, for he had had only a brief glimpse of the man coming over the barrier. "But sixteen feet for a pole vault! That's more than a world record, Tom!"

"Well, Ned, this Leopard is probably a world-beater in more ways than pole-vaulting. Anyhow, I'm glad not many can do what he did."

So the League of the Leopard was broken up, at least for the time, as the scoundrels were sent to prisons for long terms and the leader himself deported as a criminal prisoner. The anarchist accompanied him. Thus two dangerous, desperate men were put out of the way of doing further harm to Uncle Sam.

Tom was puzzled as to how the thumb prints of the Leopard's marks came to be on the windshield of Ned's car since the young manager said the black-bearded foreigner had not taken part in the actual kidnapping. It was later learned that the Leopard had gone to Ned's car after the crime, before Tom reached it, and had affixed his sinister "trademark," probably as a grim gesture of defiance.

Tom Swift received official thanks from the head of the Secret Service department in Washington for his part in helping to capture the dangerous anarchist. He was also asked to permit the use of his television detector officially, and of course this he readily gave. When it became known what sort of apparatus it was, the scientific world acclaimed the young inventor.

"There doesn't seem much left now for you to tackle," Ned remarked one day as they were talking over past events.

"Well," said Tom slowly, "I'm thinking of developing a human assimilator of congealed delights."

"What in the world is that?" asked Helen

Morton who, with Mrs. Swift, was sitting on the porch beside Tom and Ned.

"That," Tom said gravely, "is what I become when I eat an ice cream soda."

"Then let's all go assimilate some!" proposed Mrs. Swift, laughing.

And they all went.

THE END

This Isn't All!

Would you like to know what became of the good friends you have made in this book?

Would you like to read other stories continuing their adventures and experiences, or other books quite as entertaining by the same author?

On the *reverse side* of the wrapper which comes with this book, you will find a wonderful list of stories which you can buy at the same store where you got this book.

Don't throw away the Wrapper

Use it as a handy catalog of the books you want some day to have. But in case you do mislay it, write to the Publishers for a complete catalog.

THE TOM SWIFT SERIES

By VICTOR APPLETON
Author of "The Don Sturdy Series."

Every boy possesses some form of inventive genius. Tom Swift is a bright, ingenious boy and his inventions and adventures make the most interesting kind of reading.

TOM SWIFT AND HIS MOTOR CYCLE
TOM SWIFT AND HIS MOTOR BOAT
TOM SWIFT AND HIS AIRSHIP
TOM SWIFT AND HIS SUBMARINE BOAT
TOM SWIFT AND HIS WIRELESS MESSAGE
TOM SWIFT AND HIS ELECTRIC RUNABOUT
TOM SWIFT AMONG THE DIAMOND MAKERS
TOM SWIFT IN THE CAVES OF ICE
TOM SWIFT AND HIS SKY RACER
TOM SWIFT AND HIS ELECTRIC RIFLE
TOM SWIFT IN THE CITY OF GOLD
TOM SWIFT AND HIS AIR GLIDER
TOM SWIFT IN CAPTIVITY
TOM SWIFT AND HIS WIZARD CAMERA
TOM SWIFT AND HIS GREAT SEARCHLIGHT
TOM SWIFT AND HIS GIANT CANNON
TOM SWIFT AND HIS PHOTO TELEPHONE
TOM SWIFT AND HIS AERIAL WARSHIP
TOM SWIFT AND HIS BIG TUNNEL
TOM SWIFT IN THE LAND OF WONDERS
TOM SWIFT AND HIS WAR TANK
TOM SWIFT AND HIS AIR SCOUT
TOM SWIFT AND HIS UNDERSEA SEARCH
TOM SWIFT AMONG THE FIRE FIGHTERS
TOM SWIFT AND HIS ELECTRIC LOCOMOTIVE
TOM SWIFT AND HIS FLYING BOAT
TOM SWIFT AND HIS GREAT OIL GUSHER
TOM SWIFT AND HIS CHEST OF SECRETS
TOM SWIFT AND HIS AIRLINE EXPRESS
TOM SWIFT CIRCLING THE GLOBE
TOM SWIFT AND HIS TALKING PICTURES
TOM SWIFT AND HIS HOUSE ON WHEELS
TOM SWIFT AND HIS BIG DIRIGIBLE
TOM SWIFT AND HIS SKY TRAIN
TOM SWIFT AND HIS GIANT MAGNET

GROSSET & DUNLAP, Publishers, NEW YORK

THE DON STURDY SERIES
By VICTOR APPLETON
Author of "The Tom Swift Series"

Every red-blooded boy will enjoy the thrilling adventures of Don Sturdy. In company with his uncles, one a big game hunter, the other a noted scientist, he travels far and wide—into the jungles of South America, across the Sahara, deep into the African jungle, up where the Alaskan volcanoes spout, down among the head hunters of Borneo and many other places where there is danger and excitement. Every boy who has known Tom Swift will at once become the boon companion of daring Don Sturdy.

DON STURDY ON THE DESERT OF MYSTERY

DON STURDY WITH THE BIG SNAKE HUNTERS

DON STURDY IN THE TOMBS OF GOLD

DON STURDY ACROSS THE NORTH POLE

DON STURDY IN THE LAND OF VOLCANOES

DON STURDY IN THE PORT OF LOST SHIPS

DON STURDY AMONG THE GORILLAS

DON STURDY CAPTURED BY HEAD HUNTERS

DON STURDY IN LION LAND

DON STURDY IN THE LAND OF GIANTS

DON STURDY ON THE OCEAN BOTTOM

DON STURDY IN THE TEMPLES OF FEAR

GROSSET & DUNLAP, Publishers, NEW YORK